THUNDERSTORM

ALSO BY NIYAH MOORE
Pigalle Palace

Strebor
Quickiez

THUNDERSTORM

A NOVEL
NIYAH MOORE

STREBOR BOOKS
NEW YORK LONDON TORONTO SYDNEY

Strebor Books
P.O. Box 6505
Largo, MD 20792
www.simonandschuster.com

This book is a work of fiction. Names, characters, places and incidents are products of the author's imagination or are used fictitiously. Any resemblance to actual events or locales or persons, living or dead, is entirely coincidental.

© 2016 by Niyah Moore

ISBN 978-1-59309-634-2
ISBN 978-1-4767-8333-8 (ebook)
LCCN 2015957691

First Strebor Books trade paperback edition March 2016

Cover design: www.mariondesigns.com
Cover photograph: © Keith Saunders/Keith Saunders Photos

10 9 8 7 6 5 4 3 2 1

Manufactured in the United States of America

For information regarding special discounts for bulk purchases, please contact Simon & Schuster Special Sales at 1-866-506-1949

The Simon & Schuster Speakers Bureau can bring authors to your live event. For more information or to book an event, contact the Simon & Schuster Speakers Bureau at 1-866-248-3049 or visit our website at www.simonspeakers.com.

ACKNOWLEDGMENTS

First, I want to thank God because without Him, I wouldn't be blessed the way that He has blessed me. To my husband, Malcolm, thank you for loving me. You are an amazing man that has shown me that a fairytale of having a Knight in shining armor isn't too good to be true. This is our life and I love you. To my kids, Ciera, Cameron, and my angel in heaven, Londyn, I love you guys more than words can ever express. My parents, Chris, and Sharon, my sisters, Koko and Crystal, and my brother, Chris—I love you guys. To my enormous family of aunts, uncles, and cousins—I love you guys, too. It's way too many to name off the top of my head. I don't want to single anyone out.

To my best friend, Tanera, thanks for being there no matter what. Through good and bad times, we made it. To all my friends, thank you for being there when I needed you. You know who you are and there are too many to name individually, but you know who you are.

I want to send a special shout-out to my literary family: Zane, Charmaine, N'Tyse, Karen E. Quinones Miller, Shakir Rashaan, Carla Pennington, and Ambiance Books as a whole. I'm so glad that I have connected with you all. I love everyone that crosses my path, but you all have a special place in my heart.

I want to thank all the reviewers and all of the readers (#Read Moore Crew). You all have taken the time to let me know that you are out there reading my work. Without your feedback, I wouldn't be able to grow as an artist. Thank you ALL from the bottom of my heart.

COVENANT LAWS OF PIGALLE PALACE

Thou shall not release venom when biting a mortal, unless thou are ready to make her thy wife.

Thou shall not kill humans under any circumstance.

Thou shall enjoy the pleasures of Club Vaisseau, as thou please.

Thou shall not go outside the Red Light District.

Thou shall have blood slaves, but no more than one at a time.

Thou shall not go against the King.

PIGALLE PALACE TERMS

Daywalker: A Daywalker is a vampire that can walk around in the daytime without being burned by the sun.

Divination: A King shall return to rule Pigalle, crowned by King Allemand. The Divine One shall be the heir of King Allemand and Queen Christione's bloodline. The birthright was taken and shall be returned immediately. He shall be a Daywalker with extraordinary powers. Once he is proven the Divine One, the Préfet shall immediately disband and allow the King to rule the kingdom. Let no one stand in the way of what is to be.

Enchantress: An Enchantress is a witch that makes potions, spells for love, and talismans for protection.

Prototype: A Prototype is the first known vampires bitten by bats.

Pureblood: A Pureblood is a vampire born of two vampires.

Spellbinder: A Spellbinder is a witch that casts binding spells that can lead to death.

PROLOGUE

Once Rain took his throne as the King of Pigalle Palace, he and Queen Essence were adored and showered with lavish gifts by the dozens as their union was highly celebrated. Rain had fully embraced his role and Queen Essence no longer embodied the dark side. The Château had over a few hundred staff members from cooks, maids, and individual servants. The Préfet disbanded their government and allowed Rain to make all of the decisions over the city as promised. The city needed and wanted to have a King again, but not every vampire was happy about it.

The Ravens, who had proclaimed themselves as outcasts, hated the idea of having a King. They were pleased that the Préfet was gone, but they wanted the freedom to do whatever. Rain enforced that the kingdom have order and the rules of the Covenant remained. The Ravens wanted to overthrow the King by terrorizing the city.

The Ravens didn't believe in any humans being spared from their consumption so they created quite the commotion in Paris. No vampires were allowed to step foot outside the Red Light District anymore. Humans were naturally the Ravens' prey. Not only were the Ravens feasting on them, but they were also growing rapidly in number, creating a larger brood.

Rain, Onyx, Azura, and Legend's godparents were cast out of the kingdom by Rain. That was their punishment for orchestrating the betrayal. They moved to an undisclosed location and didn't make any contact. No one questioned why King Rain ordered them to leave.

Baby Ulysses had grown into a man almost instantly, it seemed. He was as handsome as his father and uncles, but his strength was incredibly and noticeably stronger and he was more muscular. He, himself, had a hard time controlling his own strength because of how fast he'd grown. Ulysses was now a force to be reckoned with, especially when he was angry. When he threw tantrums, with his fist, he could break columns in half.

Ulysses was a Pureblood—a rare breed born to two vampires. Before Ulysses, his great-grandparents, King Allemand and Queen Christione, were the only other Purebloods. Purebloods were more powerful than any other vampire. Although Ulysses was feared mostly because of his size, women found him to be irresistibly sexy. He was cruel, arrogant, insensitive, and at times, rough.

Rain trained him to be gentle, especially with women and the humans. Ulysses' vampire instincts were strong. At times, he struggled to control his hunger. He drank from thermoses of donated blood as he learned to control his urge to want to feed on and kill humans. The only thing he couldn't control was his sexual appetite. When it came to pleasing women, Ulysses was a beast. He loved manipulating their minds, making them pawns in his hands.

His parents, Onyx and Soleil, were proud of him, regardless of how many women were in and out of his bed. If anything ever happened to King Rain, Ulysses would be the next King. Ulysses was smart, fast and possessed many powers that no one had ever seen in a vampire.

Ulysses' gifts were fantastic and some had yet to be discovered. Rain kept Ulysses at close range: to monitor his behaviors and to make sure that he used his powers correctly. If he didn't utilize them in the proper way, Ulysses' powers could possibly destroy the entire kingdom. Rain stressed night and day over his nephew's powers.

CHAPTER 1

ULYSSES

The humid midsummer's evening welcomed female mortals by the dozens and I hand-selected a few of the ones I wanted to entertain for the night. My personal servant, Andreas, brought them to my bedroom and I couldn't have felt more anxious. On this night, my craving seemed more intense and I couldn't wait to satisfy it. I had what Uncle Rain liked to call an unusually large appetite for the sexiest and most beautiful women in Paris.

I didn't deny that. I could admit it. I wasn't ashamed of it at all because a part of me didn't mind wanting to be every woman's lover. Women were my addiction and I did not intend to stop anytime soon. There was no cure for what I yearned for and I didn't want one.

Women were succulent and delectable. They had a way of walking and talking that made me bite on my lower lip. The way they each carried their own heavenly scent drove me absolutely wild. There was something amazing about their ample round bottoms, soft breasts, legs, and hips. I needed to sex them the same way I needed to drink blood. Having great sex was a necessity much like getting the proper nutrition to live a long life.

Whenever a woman was in my presence, her scent would wash over me and my nostrils would flare. A young lady's blood was satisfying and so sweet-smelling and the taste of her was more delicious. I didn't like the taste of a male's blood. It was too bitter.

I compared drinking a woman's blood to drinking an alcoholic beverage. When someone felt fucked up about life and wanted to get drunk, he always reached for his favorite scotch or vodka before going for a merlot. His intentions were to get drunk quickly and that scotch or vodka would get him fucked up the quickest. Women's blood got me screwed up so fast. It was like my scotch. When I drank it, I felt so drunk. I loved the feeling.

I could smell a woman's blood from miles away. The scent was mouthwatering. *I wanted it...* I needed the delicious thick, dark-red liquid that slowly oozed out of a woman's veins down my parched throat. However, let me be clear; no matter what Uncle Rain thought, I didn't have the urge to kill anyone. That was a forbidden law of the Covenant and I had been taught well. Uncle Rain acted as if one day my urge would become greater than my desire and I would do the unimaginable. *Killing wasn't my thing.* I didn't like it. I didn't like how dark it made me feel on the inside. I had accidentally killed a woman once when I was drunk. The darkness loomed over me for weeks. I was capable of killing, but I wouldn't dare. He could give me some credit there.

As I grew into a man, I became fully aware of the kind of pleasure I could give to a woman. It wasn't sucking the blood that had my adrenaline rushing. A woman's beauty was like art and I was the painter—a true artist who was in love with his craft. I could detect a woman's beauty, not only from the outside, but I could see what was inside of her as well. I could determine what type of woman she was before she could utter one single word. Attraction started within and it enhanced her outer appearance.

While listening to the four women that I had in my company for the night, I paid close attention to the way they were laughing. The highs and lows of their giggles let me know that they were truly having a great time, drinking pink Moscato wine, and eating the hors d'oeuvres I had picked out for them. Other than the treats, they were also enjoying stealing stares at me. I was in the corner, relaxing on a plush chair, sipping champagne, and watching them quietly.

One woman called me Chocolate Heaven once. I laughed at that title when I first heard it, but it was as if she had passed that name along because she wasn't the last to say it. Each one uttered it as if it was the code word they needed for me to let them into my world. It was quite adorable to me. I didn't consider myself chocolate in color. Rain was more like chocolate. I was brown like cocoa. Chocolate was chocolate, I guessed.

My mysterious silence always intrigued women and it seemed as if my demeanor fascinated them. They were waiting for me to say something, but I was going to make them wait. It was like a game of cat and mouse. I would let them run around freely, but then pounce on them when I was ready. I leaned back and continued to listen to the sounds of their delightful laughter. Their laughter was much needed and their smiling faces helped to make my heavy thoughts dissipate.

After the long, drawn-out meeting I'd had with my family earlier that day, I was left feeling as if I needed an escape from what was going on in the Red Light District. Yet, another dead human body had been found in the alley near Club Vaisseau and I didn't like to think about it. That was all Uncle Rain could talk about and I was growing sick of it. Rain was the King. How come he wasn't making any arrests? The Ravens were the ones killing and we knew it, so why weren't we going after them and making them pay for making the Red Light District dangerous? How was he going to stop bodies from turning up in the Red Light District if he never left the Palace? It was stupid to me. He was letting them be and we were to go on with our own lives as if it wasn't happening. It was

Uncle Rain's duty to keep the district safe for all and he was failing miserably at it. He hadn't come up with a single solution to how he was going to stop the killings. All he was doing was talking about it.

Uncle Legend and my father did what they were told without many rebuttals. Aunt Azura was opposite. She was usually the most vocal in our family meetings. She didn't hide how she was feeling. I was with her when she said that the only way to fix the problem was to kill the Ravens and take control of the club again. The club was out of control and the killings never happened when the family was running it. Ever since our family had abandoned Vaisseau, the Ravens had taken it over, used it as a recruiting headquarters, and they were starting to terrorize any human that came down to the Red Light District.

The Ravens were joined by the old brood that Essence had created when she was confused about her being. They were lost newborns and couldn't control their thirst for mortal blood so they joined the Ravens. They had a brand-new leader, some guy named Claude Parrish, and he was definitely letting every vampire know that if the Ravens wanted to, they could hunt and kill. The Ravens were doing more than breaking the laws of the Covenant. They were trying to start a war. Rain had warned us all to stay far away from the club because it was too dangerous. He was going to take care of it when the time was right. In the meantime, we were going to have to keep listening to him rant every time a body turned up.

I couldn't listen to it anymore. I was going to continue to do only the things I loved doing—*pleasuring women*. That was all I needed. Women were a great distraction to help take my mind off being the Prince of a destiny I didn't want.

I had gotten up from the chair and leaned up against the wall to continue to watch the women drink more wine and converse freely. I was going to speak soon enough. I intended to drink a little from each of them. I was going to nibble a little, much like a snack, and they were going to love me for it. I was a damn good lover, and in return, women allowed me to drink from them at free will. My enormous appetite and high sexual desire allowed me to please each one of them all night long; the way I liked it.

I was stubborn and a little rebellious. Uncle Rain ruled Pigalle Palace with his heart on his sleeve and it took him a long time to walk in his birthright prior to taking the throne. Truthfully, I still thought he was too soft to be a King. Those were my thoughts and though it felt wrong to feel that way about my own Uncle, I wasn't going to be in denial about it. This kingdom needed an iron fist.

When and if I ever got the chance to rule over Pigalle Palace, I would do things the way they should be. In the meantime, I didn't need to fulfill any royal duties. Rain was still the King and as long as he was the King, which would be forever, I was going to continue doing whatever I wanted.

My cell phone buzzed against my hip. I checked it. It was my mother texting, telling me to send the women home because Rain was on his way to shut my party down. I didn't reply to the text. I hated it when she tried to tell me what to do as if I were a child. I wasn't harming anyone, so I didn't see why my entertaining was such a big deal.

I glanced across the room and noticed one of them was extremely attractive. She stood out like a vivid red rose sitting in a dead rose garden. She was now sitting alone at the end of the couch, away from the others. She appeared to be very confident as she stared back at me. The chandelier above her was glimmering off her dark-brown eyes, making them sparkle. I was fixated on her. Her roasted almond-colored skin almost looked as if she was dipped in candy coating.

Taking a good look at her, the thought of having sex instantly electrified me. Aroused by the possibility of what I could do to her, I approached her slowly. This lovely, curvy, wide-eyed beauty was such a distraction that the others faded from the room. I couldn't take my eyes off her. I made up in my mind to send the others home to have her all to myself.

As I barely raised my right hand, I signaled to my servant, Andreas, and he came to me.

"Yes, your highness?" he asked.

"I want her. Send the others home in a few minutes."

Andreas bowed his head and replied, "Yes, your highness."

I wasn't in the mood to entertain them all. I only wanted that particular one. That was a rare thing. One woman never actually could curb my large desire, but I was willing to try something new.

While Andreas was delivering my message to the others, so many thoughts ran through my mind. I thought of taking a sip of her sweet young blood first before fucking her. Her delicious scent had me ready and my fangs began to elongate as my thoughts began to run wild with me.

The woman standing before me nearly shuddered as I lightly grazed her chin with the tips of my fingers. *What was it about this heavenly mortal that I found so intriguing?* I was going to find out.

"Hello," I finally said.

"Hello. It's sweet of you to finally speak, Chocolate Heaven," she said with a shy grin and a giggle.

"Aren't you something," I stated with a smile forming.

The temptation I felt to devour this woman on the spot was astounding to me. I was standing in front of her while she was still sitting, admiring her long, curly, black hair, and I suddenly felt the need to run my fingers through it.

Before I could get my hands into her hair, she immediately rose to her feet and she stood about five feet five inches in height. I stood around six feet tall, so while I stared down at her, I got a good look at her firm breasts trying to pop out of her V-neck blouse. Her black miniskirt accentuated her thick legs.

Yes! I wanted her badly.

"I was waiting for the right time to come and say hello," I flirted.

Bursting into the room with a loud bang of the door, Uncle Rain didn't attempt to cloak his presence or give me the respect a man should get while having company. The other women hadn't made it out of the door yet.

Everyone faced him and all talking and laughing ceased immediately as their bodies tensed up, becoming like a herd of deer caught in the headlights of an oncoming car. They looked unsure whether or not to make a dash for it.

"Get the fuck out!" he shouted with his fangs elongated and exposed.

As the women quickly scurried out of the door, I groaned, "You gotta be kiddin' me…"

With a parting glance, I memorized the beautiful woman's face, hoping I would see her again sooner than later.

She was gone that quickly.

I flashed my uncle a hard glare. His eyes were back on mine with fire in them. He didn't utter another word. The disgusted snarl on his face led me to believe that he'd had enough of my rebellious spirit. He marched out of my room.

I propelled air from my lips and crossed my arms over my chest. I wanted to throw a tantrum, but I was no longer a child. I was a man and I wanted to be treated like one. Uncle Rain had ruined my party for the night. I was frustrated. My parents were going to have that talk with me again about my purpose and I was going to do my best not to go off.

I didn't give a fuck about my purpose. All I wanted to do was to find the beautiful stranger, and the next time, I was going to have her all to myself. If Uncle Rain wanted things this way, then fine. I was going to conduct my business away from the Château from now on, even if it was in Paris.

CHAPTER 2

RAIN

A fter ending Ulysses' little private party, I headed to my bedroom, feeling as if I was going to have to do something about his respect for me. The mansion was so large that anyone would get lost in the never-ending set of hallways and doors. Huge paintings of our grandparents, King Allemand and Queen Christione, were displayed on one of the walls near my bedroom. There was one single painting of our mother as a child in the middle. That painting was the most sacred to me. I stopped to stare at it every time I passed it. I looked into her eyes to see her soul. Through the painting, I could tell that she hated being different. Her birth defect of being human was her curse.

I wished she were still alive to tell me everything. I stared at her picture and wondered what our lives would've been like if she hadn't been murdered. After a few moments of thinking, I stared at her picture and proceeded to my bedroom. Overlooking the window of our bedroom, my wife stood. Essence looked radiant and perfect as always. Her mocha-colored skin and her ebony tamed curls were flowing down the middle of her back. It was an incredibly warm night and the stars were shining above, decorating the sky the way bright lights did on a Christmas tree.

All of the windows were covered with thick red curtains to block the sunlight. I wound up having all the windows covered with UV protection as soon as we'd moved in. That way everyone could enjoy the sun if they desired, but the curtains remained because they were hand-made by our grandmother, Queen Christione.

I loved it when Essence would stand there and look on as if she thought the sky was the most beautiful thing in the world. She also enjoyed watching the waterfront after spending the whole day roaming the Château and interacting with other vampires, who came to her for advice and encouragement.

We were solitary creatures by nature and didn't trust anyone. Being a vampire wasn't easy and Essence had a way of making other vampires feel comforted as she helped them with whatever problems they were having. Some were dealing with their transition and some were tired of living with the curse. She taught them that they could call upon her for help anytime they needed her. She was the perfect Queen and they loved her, but I loved her more because she had evolved into everything I ever imagined.

"Essence…"

She turned and faced me with a look of worry nestled in her almond-shaped eyes. "Yes, my King."

I felt relieved once we were married. My lonely existence had changed and I would no longer go another century without my soul mate. Essence was my soul-bonded mate and she held my heart tightly with her own. She kept it safe and protected it. She was my one *true* love and I was now a complete being. It didn't matter if the bond was once broken when she slept with my brother. She was in a confused state and she was remorseful. They both were.

While gazing upon her, I wanted to forget about what was going on in the Red Light District, but I couldn't. More bodies were turning up left and right. The Ravens were maliciously murdering more humans by the day. I had yet to meet their new leader, Claude Parish. His followers feared him so much that they were doing whatever he wanted them to do. Vampires were designed to be monsters, but that was why I tried so hard to enforce the Covenant. Vampires needed rules in order to be civilized. We needed rules to coexist with humans.

It would only be a matter of time before the Ravens' lust for blood was going to become permanent, and the need for more blood would spread if I didn't do something about it. The Ravens were going to try to wipe out the human race in Montmartre and they were going at it hard.

The Red Light District was supposed to be the place where tourists came to enjoy sex and maybe fulfill their curiosity about us. Once they realized that they were on the brink of extinction, the vampires would no longer be a dark mystery and they were going to have to fight back. We would be looked at as evil abominations that needed to be hunted, in turn, and destroyed.

"I'm going to have to try to talk to this new leader of the Ravens," I sighed.

Essence inhaled and exhaled lightly. "I have a feeling it may be a very violent situation if the conversation goes wrong… I hear Claude Parish isn't an easy man to talk to. Do you need me to come with you?"

She would kill for me as I would kill for her. That was such a sexy thing, but I wasn't going to let her put herself in harm's way.

"No… Let me handle it."

"As the King, you have every right to make arrests and threaten a few death sentences. They shouldn't get away with defying your wishes."

I sighed with a deep breath.

Essence touched me lightly on the shoulder. "You'll work this out, love, but if you want, I'll ride with you."

"You're my rider… I love that." My eyes roamed her body.

She was wearing a white nightgown made of the finest silk and it molded her curves and stopped mid-thigh. I could see her nipples that looked like chocolate-covered morsels through the thin material as it draped over her beautifully formed breasts.

Once my eyes traveled back up to her face, we locked eyes. She could sense the heat and arousal in my gaze.

She smiled confidently and whispered against my lips, "You are the vampire's King, but you are truly *my* King. If you need me, you know I have your back."

I kissed her and kept my arms around her as I stared out of the window. The countryside on the other side of the Château had been warm at that time of the night. When it was daytime, I enjoyed how the sun made it vibrant with the scent of summer still lingering, but with the fresh promise of autumn's breeze. In the winter, frost covered the hard ground. The trees would be naked, shivering against the blue sky as the wind blew past it. That's what I loved most about being a Daywalker. I got to enjoy nature's beauty.

I wanted Essence to enjoy it with me, but she couldn't. All she had were her memories. Her skin would no longer touch the sun ever again. She could only stare from behind UV-protected glass with sad eyes. I noticed she hardly ever did without bursting into tears.

I stated, "I have your back as well."

She squeezed me tightly. "Thank you."

I savored our intimate embrace by tilting my head down and kissing her lips with so much passion. Her lips were always sweet and could take my mind off a million problems. I let my hand wander her body, touching every place that turned her on.

Slowly, my hands went under her long gown and I caressed her soft thighs. She wrapped one leg around my waist, pressing herself up against me. We kissed for what felt like hours, but surely, it had only been a few seconds. Our kisses were interrupted by a loud knock on the door before I could get her naked.

We parted and she smiled.

"Yes?" I scowled and called out.

One of the servants entered and bowed before us. "Excuse me, but your bath is ready, Queen Essence."

"Thank you," Essence replied and then stared at me. "I'll see you later." She placed another sweet kiss on my lips before leaving to take her bath.

It didn't matter how many times I stared at that woman as she walked away with that mean switch in her walk. I still felt like I was staring at her for the first time when I met her at Club Vaisseau.

CHAPTER 3

LEGEND

"Come, Legend… I need you," a voice whispered loudly in my ear as I floated away from my dream.

I sat up in my bed bare-chested. Glancing over at the clock, I saw that it was eight o'clock in the evening. The sun hadn't set that long ago and it was time for me to get up. I was having yet another crazy dream, but this dream seemed to come to life.

It was *she* again.

I had never seen this woman's face before, but her voice was always clear. She had been calling me for weeks without a glimpse of what she looked like. I was beginning to have doubts about her existence, but each time, the dream became more real than the last. This woman had to be more than a whispery voice that was haunting me.

In my dreams, I was running toward her voice, searching frantically. When I thought I was headed in the right direction, her voice would come from another direction, and I would go running toward it. I had yet to find her. It was like a wild goose chase and I was becoming frustrated every time I woke up to realize it was only a dream. What did the dream mean? Was it supposed to be interpreted?

Why was she calling me? Why was I chasing her?

I removed a few dreads that had fallen in my face and tied them behind my neck. My heart was pumping hard and the sweat was dripping from my entire body, so much that it had saturated the sheets. I got up and removed the wet sheets roughly, tossing them to the floor in frustration.

The woman without a face was surely haunting me and I couldn't take it anymore.

I breathed acutely, chest heaving in and out, angrily as I realized I would never get to see her.

"It's a dream," I said to myself aloud.

Suddenly, the familiar voice filled my bedroom. *"Come to me... Legend."*

Her voice was usually soft and faint while I was sleeping, but now her voice seemed louder and I was wide awake. I blinked my eyes and rubbed them to make sure I wasn't still dreaming.

I looked around my large bedroom to see if I could see her, hiding somewhere, playing a game of hide-and-seek. No one was there, but me. My mind had officially fucked me up. Who was she? I had to know.

"Please come to me... Legend." Her voice came again.

She always had a hint of sexual desire for me whenever she said my name. A surge of energy from the sound of her voice sent a shiver down my spine.

She was driving me insane.

"Who are you?" I questioned loudly. I waited. There was no reply. "Are you going to finally reveal yourself to me? Or are you going to keep torturing me?"

I tried to narrow in on our mental connection. She was indeed another vampire, one that was strong enough to tap into my mind without being in front of me. She sounded as if she were very distant and weak, almost as if her blood were being depleted.

My instinct, to protect this woman, shook me. Her pain and her need became mine for whatever reason. How was our connection so strong, yet we had never met?

"*Legend, you must come to me.*"

I looked up at the ceiling. "Where are you?"

I waited to hear her response. I closed my eyes and zoned in on our connection.

She said, "*The Caribbean Islands...*"

My heart sped up. She finally gave some sort of location. I couldn't fight the seductress' call any longer. Where in the Caribbean was she? I tried to tap into her to locate her, but her connection was far too weak. Her voice floated away, away to nothing. Our connection was gone and I was left with the mystery of her, again. It was yet another day of not knowing why she was calling me to help her.

I groaned as my hand rubbed my face. I was going to have to find out who she was and what she wanted from me before I drove myself crazy.

Being the oldest brother, without a mate, I had a few female vampires fighting for my affection constantly, but I was waiting for the perfect time to settle down. There was something about this mysterious woman. Her way of reaching me through psychic connection was definitely unique and undeniable. Could she be the one?

I couldn't search for her when I didn't know her name, where she was, or if she were real. What if this was some crazy fantasy, I was having? I had a yearning for her and I didn't know why. I suddenly felt strange. I felt something evil lurking in the dark depth of the shadows of her. Every time she called after me, the unknown presence of her felt closer and became more suffocating. Each time, I felt she was in serious trouble.

I was going to have to go to the Caribbean Islands. Our connection would be that much stronger if I went. Then, maybe, I would be able to find her. I hoped it would be nothing like the dreams I had because I wasn't going to keep chasing her to a dead-end.

As I stepped over the sheets that were on the floor, I went and showered. I got dressed and took a good look at the way the night's sky was covered with stars from my opened balcony door. I tried not to let my emotions cloud my mind as I thought carefully.

This female vampire could've been in danger... Or that's what it felt like to me. Every cell in my body was telling me that I needed to protect her—no matter what. I had never felt that feeling before, not even for my first wife, Chantal. She had been my only wife and was dead now. She was never my soul mate. She was never supposed to be mine. That was the reason why she was murdered. I had to live with that for the rest of my immortal life.

I wished Onyx and Rain had never told me about the intensity they felt when they found their soul mates. My feelings toward women had always been warm, never on fire. Was this the feeling they were talking about? If so, then I understood why they stopped at nothing to be with them. Now, I was burning for a woman who was visiting me through my hallucinations. She had eluded my dreams and called my name through psychic communication as if I already belonged to her.

Taking a deep breath, I tried to gain control of the feelings, but it wasn't working. I was going to have to have a discussion with my family before going to the Caribbean.

Our parents that raised us, though they weren't our birth parents, were banned from the kingdom and I had no idea where they were. They had been my guides and I couldn't ask them to give me advice about this. Rain was King and we were by his side, supporting every decision he made, so I was going to have to lean on him.

Reaching for my cell phone, I sent my siblings a group text to let them know that I would be leaving shortly. They usually woke up around this time anyway, so they were already up and moving around. Rain, well, he hardly ever slept, so he was always awake.

They entered my room, literally, seconds after I sent the emergency text.

Rain arrived first with his usual King flare, quickly before I could put the cell phone back on the dresser. Ever since he had become King, he traded his T-shirts for tunics. He wore a crown, cloak, black pants, and boots. His attire spoke everything of a modern king. He was our leader and very confident in his role. There was nothing subtle about his transformation whatsoever. He was a true King and I admired that about him.

Onyx walked in with confusion written all over his face in his blue jeans and gray sweater. He usually moved without being heard. The average human would never be able to hear him enter a room. As the father of Ulysses and husband of Soleil, he was a great protector of his family.

Azura was last to arrive, but not too long after them. Her presence was soft, as always, but was an active force nevertheless as she strutted in tight leather pants, black corset, and spiked heels. Her way of reading minds was annoying, so I immediately blocked her out of my head. I didn't want her to start going off about how chasing a woman would lead to my own destruction. I was in control of my own fate. That was why I hated premonitions.

All of their eyes pierced through me, waiting for me to say why I was leaving in such a hurry. I was afraid my siblings would think I was crazy to go like this for a woman that only whispered to me in my dreams. I had spoken about her before, but they told me to ignore her. We didn't know what this woman wanted, so why go seeking for the unknown? At that moment, their unity and intensity nearly intimidated me. But, no matter what, I was the oldest brother. Whether Rain was King or not, I still had a right to say what was on my mind.

I stood straight with my head held high in the air. "I'm glad you all could come to see me before I leave."

Azura took a seat in the corner of the room. "Whenever you block me out of your mind, it must be serious... Where are you going?"

"The lady Vamp... She spoke to me again. This time, I was awake. I'm going to find her," I replied.

Rain asked in a firm deep tone, "Has she told you where she was?"

I dared not to clench my teeth while answering, "No. She said she was in the Caribbean. That's it."

"That could be any place," Rain replied.

I cut him off, "She's in some sort of trouble. She's weak and I think she's in some kind of trouble."

"She's unable to get blood," Azura said. "That's why she's so weak. She needs blood, but not any kind of blood. She needs royal blood."

"Who is she?" I asked since Azura seemed to know so much all of a sudden.

Rain looked as if he had no clue. He was waiting for what Azura had to say while Onyx shrugged.

"Her name is Mirage Oleander," Azura stated. "She's been called MiMi here and there. She's the last living Prototype."

"I haven't heard the term 'Prototype' in ages," I said.

Our godparents were the last ones to speak of Prototypes, but they never went into any detail. All we knew was that they were extinct.

Azura continued, "There were six Prototypes originally, three female and three males. They were the first vampires to live."

"How were they created?" I asked.

"They were attacked and bitten by bats. The Prototypes created the first two Purebloods. One was King Allemand born from one set and Queen Christine of another set. They had been the only Purebloods before Ulysses was born. Our mother should've been the purest of a Pureblood, but she was born human... Well, you know the rest..."

"Wait, did you say the Prototype's name is Mirage?" Rain asked.

"Yes. You heard of her?" Azura replied.

"I was told she was dead. The Préfet said that all of the Proto-types were killed including Mirage Oleander."

"Well, she is still very much alive, but barely," Azura said.

"How do you know?" Rain asked with narrowed suspicious eyes.

"Relax. I'm not hiding anything from you so don't you start pick-ing at me. It came to me in a premonition yesterday. I didn't speak on it because I thought I had to be crazy, but I can feel her. I'm sure the Préfet hoped she was dead for whatever reasons."

"What the hell does she want with me?" I asked with wide eyes.

"Legend, it's something I can't put my finger on. I'm sure that word has traveled that a living descendant of Allemand has taken the throne," she replied.

"Well, I called you all here to tell you that I can no longer wait." I paced the floor. "My desire to protect her is high... I want to find her..."

My siblings exchanged uncomfortable glances.

"Legend, you want me to give you permission to leave?" Rain questioned.

I hated it when he thought I was asking for permission. True, he was the King, but I was the oldest son. If he would've told me no, I would've gone anyway and dealt with the consequences later. I never questioned the Divination when we discovered that I wasn't a Daywalker on my twenty-first birthday. Of course, I was disap-pointed because, as the oldest, it should've been my destiny to be the heir to the throne. But, it wasn't my destiny; it was my baby brother's. I learned to swallow that jealousy a long time ago.

"I'm simply letting you know where I'm going, so you can be aware of my whereabouts."

Rain didn't appear to be too upset or worried much as he stared at me. He replied, "Find her and bring her to me. I need to talk with her. Anything out of the ordinary when you reach her, you have to be prepared to do whatever it takes to bring her back here in one piece. It is my duty to keep the only living Prototype alive. I wouldn't want Claude and his Ravens to get ahold of her first."

"I got it."

"Who knows if this is some kind of trap, so keep that in mind too."

"Why would it be some kind of trap?" I questioned.

"Don't question me. There are too many unanswered questions surrounding the murders of our grandparents and parents... I'm still trying to figure it all out. The Prototypes were here before any of us were. Mirage holds the knowledge that we need. If someone tried to kill her, that means they are in fear of the information that she can bring to me," he made clear.

I nodded. What he said made sense. Too many things about our existence were confusing enough, and I was sure that Mirage had all of the answers.

Rain motioned for Onyx and Azura to follow him out of my bedroom.

I got ready to embark on my trip to find Mirage.

CHAPTER 4

AZURA

"Why is Legend chasing her? Does he think she was supposed to be his soul mate or something?" I questioned Rain and Onyx as we walked down the corridor of the Château.

"We have to wait and see," Rain barked.

This shit was crazy and he was a fool. For whatever reason, MiMi was supposed to be dead and no one was questioning how she was surviving. It was all too funny style to me. I had a feeling that this was more than trying to save a depleted Prototype. Legend was falling in love with her before meeting her but, of course, Legend wasn't going to listen to anybody's warnings. All the men in this family seemed to be hardheaded when it came to women.

Since I didn't know what the deal was with her, I wasn't going to speak on it anymore. I was going to wait and see what kind of mess this would create. I was a bit sour and bitter when it came to looking for love because I didn't believe in going after and chasing anyone. Love was supposed to find you. Rain and Onyx both pursued their wives. They were happy and in love now, so I got that, but Legend hadn't been so lucky in that department. I didn't put myself in situations to fall in love, so I didn't have some bad boyfriend love drama of my own. Maybe that was why I was so bitter. Where was my Prince Charming? Did I want a Prince? I loved women far too much to give up my lifestyle.

Rain wanted all of us to find love eventually. He claimed it was the best feeling. I, on the other hand, thought love was for suckers. I fucked around with whomever I wanted. My indiscretions weren't a secret and my brothers never questioned whom I slept with. They never had. As long as I was there for my brothers to support them, that was all that mattered to them.

I didn't have the time or the energy to entertain the idea of any type of relationship. What I needed was a quickie. A "no strings attached" type of situation. That was suitable for me and kept me satisfied. I had no burning desire to find a wife. The word "eternity" sounded dreadful.

Rain told me once that an empty existence without love would wear me down. I wasn't worried about feeling empty because I didn't feel empty yet. Sex calmed me down from time to time and it gave me a release.

I was okay with sex, but with all these new rules in place, it left me a little time to get my groove on. I hated all these new regulations. It was tough enough abiding by the rules of the Covenant. The moment the Préfet stepped down, I felt like it was going to mean freedom, but I was wrong. Rain kept every single rule in place. Once Rain banned us from going to Vaisseau because he felt it wasn't for the royal family, I felt like I was a prisoner in my own home.

Fuck all that. I felt much like Ulysses had. I wanted to be able to go out and hang out, get drunk, fuck, and do it all over again the next day. I didn't see anything wrong with it. Not everyone wanted to be with one person for the rest of his or her lives.

I parted ways from Onyx and Rain and headed to my own bedroom. I got dressed up in my black spandex mini dress and high "fuck me" boots that came up to my knees. I curled my long hair and put on some red lipstick, grabbed my coat, and headed out of the Château. As much as Rain wanted us stay away from Club

Vaisseau, I wasn't going to stay away anymore. It was the only place vampires got together to have a good time. Honestly, if there were some other vampire club, I wouldn't have gone because Vaisseau was like my second home. We built that place from the ground up.

I was ready to hunt for some exciting action to get away from being between the boring palace walls.

I walked out of the Château and no one asked me where I was going. I went out of the Kingdom's jurisdiction as I took a cab over to the club for old time's sake. There was no need to drive my Porsche or have a driver take me in a limo. It only felt right to take a cab. I missed traveling that way. As soon as the taxi drove up into the alley and pulled up in front of the club, I felt excited. I paid the fare and hopped out.

I looked at that line and smirked. There was no way I was going to wait in line. I walked right up to the bouncer and seduced him with my smile. He took one look at me and let me in, but he managed to swat my ass very quick as I passed him. I winked at him and walked into the club. If he weren't working the door, I would've taken advantage of him. If he was lucky, I would come back later.

The pounding music and red flashing lights hit me hard and it felt like I could breathe again. I closed my eyes and felt the pulse of Vaisseau fill me. I really missed this place. The smell of cigarette smoke, liquor, and sweat from the go-go dancers permeated the room. Bodies were grinding on top of one another, ready to get down and dirty at any given moment, but something was different.

Though the old Vaisseau used to be raunchy most nights, it was still an upscale nightclub that catered to singles and couples who were looking to watch or be watched, serving both humans and supernatural beings. We loved to keep it that way, but now the vibe had changed because the Ravens had changed it.

I opened my eyes and I almost wished I hadn't come. This was no longer home. This was something else. I could see a few vampires actually feeding on humans while on the dance floor. My godparents would've thrown them out immediately if they were here. I turned my eyes away in disgust. It took everything in me not to go over there and speak my mind. It wasn't my place anymore. I would be outnumbered. There were too many Ravens under one roof for me to handle on my own. I couldn't point any of them out, but I could feel their power.

I immediately noticed the lights above me were multicolored. The red lights were gone. Where did that horrible silver disco ball come from? The ceiling also had mirrors. Things definitely had changed. I wasn't sure if I liked the way it looked. I was happy to see that the wall-sized water fountain that ran behind the bar was still there.

As I was feeling a little happy about it, a very handsome blond bartender was working the bar and caught my attention. His hazel eyes were piercing through me and his skin was as white as snow. Before I could really focus on him, I moved my eyes over to the winding staircase that led upstairs to the private rooms where people went to engage in sexual activities. I smiled to see that those rooms were still used for those purposes as well.

If I couldn't enjoy the ambiance, at least I would be able to get a good fuck. My nipples instantly hardened at the thought.

I stared back at the bartender as I made my way to the bar.

As soon as I sat, he asked, "What are you doing here, tonight? Long time no see."

I paused for a moment. I had never seen him in my life, yet he spoke to me as if we knew one another. I took a good look at him. He didn't look familiar. I tried not to show my confusion with how comfortable he was with his question, but my face couldn't hide it.

Shrugging, I replied, "I needed to come and check out the new Vaisseau. I'm sorry... Have we met before?"

He smiled devilishly, refusing to answer my question. "What can I get you?"

Though he wasn't familiar and he wasn't going to tell me whether we'd met or not, I replied, "Let me get a Vodka Tonic, please."

Another deeper male voice came from behind me. "No champagne for you, tonight? Now, that's not like you."

I turned to face him. This man was gorgeous with his pale white skin, dark brown hair, and his mysterious icy blue eyes made him look a little evil. That's what I liked most about him. I had never seen him a day in my life, so how did he know what I wanted to drink? I figured he and the bartender were both Ravens. It seemed like the Ravens had been doing a little homework on me. Interesting.

He quickly introduced himself when he read my confusion, "I'm Claude Parish, the new owner of this place."

Yes, Claude Parish, he wasn't only the new club owner, but he was also the leader of the Ravens. I heard about him but hadn't had a face to put to the name. Now, I wasn't going to forget what he looked like. He was the one that kept the Ravens rebelling and behaving like wild beasts. He was our enemy.

My first thought was that he was much taller than I thought he would be as he stood a little over six feet. My second thought was more along the lines of *oh shit*...

I was so enraptured by him that I nearly got lost in my own thoughts.

I rapidly snapped out of it and introduced myself, "I'm Azura Toussaint—"

"Yes, I know who you are, Princess Azura. We have royalty in the house, tonight. To what do I owe you this pleasure? Your drinks are on the house. I must say you're more stunning up close and personal."

He was charming as he was bearing down on me with his lovely blue eyes. Though he wasn't like any other man I had ever come across, I played him off coolly.

"Is that so?"

"Someone whispered in my ear that you were here the moment you walked through the front door. I decided to come over and welcome you, myself. You like what I've done to your old place?"

My lips formed into a snarl. "I hate it."

He smiled at my comment and had the nerve to chuckle. "That's really too bad. I like it much better now. I've heard nothing but great things about it so far. Vampires feel so free...without rules..."

My eyes were back on his. I didn't want to show him how much I hated the rules, but it was as if he already knew and that was the reason why he was saying it.

The bartender finished my drink. Claude picked it up, handed it to me, and smiled. My, he was handsome. Claude watched me carefully as I sipped. My eyes weren't the only things that had his attention. His eyes gazed at the way my short dress clung to my thighs. I held in my grin.

I walked away from him with my drink in my hand. I could still feel his eyes on me as I began to dance in the sea of sweaty bodies. It seemed like all eyes were on me as I danced alone. They wanted to fuck me. Some women looked as if they wanted to fuck me too. I felt so sexy and wanted by everyone in the building that my thoughts of how horrible this place had become left me.

I swayed my hips as I felt the music and I didn't have a care in the world. The energy, the good music, sex, and everything else were still pumping through this place. I was happy that at least those things hadn't changed about it. It was everything I wanted and needed. To be away from the Château and away from my family felt right as I danced on that floor with ease.

When I slowly opened my eyes, I could see Claude coming straight to me with a slow and steady stride. His walk made me want to moan. I didn't budge or run. I wasn't afraid of him though he was a little bit intimidating. He actually stirred my curiosity. I yearned to release my sexuality that night, and if it had to be him that I released it with, I was going to be asking for trouble.

Trouble excited me and I wanted more of it.

Claude's energy spelled out that he was dominant and sex was something he wanted to give me from the moment he laid eyes on me. I could tell that right off. His rugged, dominating presence commanded my attention and as he stood in front of me, I trembled. His approach was stronger than I thought it would be. With his captivating blue eyes and dark hair, he looked as if he could've been from the United States. I was sure that when he was a mortal, he might've had a tan from playing in the sun at the beach all day to give off a radiant glow. His now hard and cold eyes warned me that he was indeed a predator and he was making me his prey.

That more than excited me; he was making me horny.

Tonight, there was only one thing he wanted... *Me.*

I kept dancing as he stood behind me. I danced up to him and he didn't back away. His strong arms wrapped around my waist and his hands were nearly climbing up my mini dress. His muscular chest was pressed up against my back and I felt like my pilot had been lit. I was on fire.

"Look at me," he demanded as he spun me around to face him.

I drank what was left in my glass before looking up at him. "What do you want?"

I was going to play hard to get. There would be no easy way to me, no matter how fine he was. I had never had sex with a white boy before and I didn't discriminate, but it was definitely the sweetest taboo.

"What do I want?" he repeated.

"Yes, what do you want?" I fluttered my eyelashes at him.

"I should be asking you that same question... Do you wish to get into somethin' wild tonight, Azura? Is that why you're here? Tell me, *mon amour*."

I shivered at the thought of him taking me right there on that dance floor and fucking my brains out while the whole club watched in excitement. He was trying to control me with seduction. My sexual desires were strong, but my loyalty to my brother was that little angel on my shoulder reminding me of the reality. Claude was the enemy.

"We've walked along two very different paths. There are too many bodies turning up in these alleyways since you've arrived on the scene. The Red Light District has never been this dangerous.... We have you to thank for that."

He ignored my way of getting him to confess his sins while he shook his head at me. "How do you want me?" he asked.

Claude was trying to elude me and I didn't like it one bit. To be able to say he had a piece of me would be perfect bragging rights. Rain would be furious. I tried to walk away, but he grabbed my wrist firmly.

"Finish dancing with me, beauty."

I removed his hands as if he was hot to my touch, but that didn't stop his body from staying in my personal space.

"As much as your aggression is a turn-on to me, I would never fuck you," I enunciated.

"No matter what you think about me or the Ravens, you have no idea what I'm doing. All you see are the things I want you to see. We are only living the way vampires were meant to live. The rules that the government put on us were never supposed to be carried out by a King. A King that doesn't make his own regulations is useless. The Préfet created those laws to control us. A King should set his own rules and allow us to be exactly what we naturally are...bloodthirsty hunters that need living prey."

"Humans aren't our prey. We aren't animals, yet your brood has been behaving like wild beasts making the streets of Paris too dangerous. Humans aren't our enemies, Claude. Yes, they have what we need to survive, but if you keep killing them, you will have to face Rain. His punishments shouldn't be taken lightly. He is the King."

"Is that supposed to be a threat? What is King Rain doing these days? We haven't seen or heard from him since he has taken his throne. Let me guess, he's too busy with his own life to protect his people?"

"You don't know my brother. I suggest that you keep your brood under control. This club should be a place for fun, sex, and more sex.... There are other ways to get blood. Killing isn't necessary."

"Other means like what? Blood slaves and blood drives? That's ancient. Haven't you ever wanted to suck blood until they become lifeless? It gives such a pleasant rush. It's a natural trait in us. Why suppress what we naturally want to do?"

While vampires were killers by nature, we didn't *have* to kill. When we ran the club, we committed ourselves to making sure no one killed for fresh blood. We had donors, so we quenched the thirst for fresh blood that way. Vampires were hunters, but Rain was making sure to keep up with the rules that the government had in place to make sure that no war against the humans would commence.

There were curious humans, who were looking for the vampire experience any day of the week. Vaisseau had always been the place that linked willing human donors with vampires, but Claude was ending their lives without warning and seemed like he was doing it to get Rain's attention.

"Look at that," Claude said, pointing to the other side of the room.

I glanced over to see a vampire fucking a mortal woman up against the wall. He was sucking the blood from her neck as he pumped into her at the same time. The woman was writhing in ecstasy against the wall and it turned me on. Thoughts of Claude doing that same thing to me bombarded me.

With his mouth resting on the edge of my ear, Claude asked, "What do you think about that?"

I shook the image. "It's been a pleasure having this conversation with you, but I must get going. I've seen enough here, tonight."

I walked away from the gorgeous, dangerous man. As much as I wanted to let our attraction to one another consume me, I fled from him. Though I wanted and needed to feel him inside of me, my loyalty overpowered.

Before I could make it off the dance floor, Claude grabbed the nape of my neck and pushed his long fingers through my hair. He had more power than I wanted him to have. The dark leader of the Ravens wasn't backing down. I felt myself lean back to give him what he wanted. He seemed pleased by my submission, and the Alpha in him was left breathless at the sight of my smooth breasts that were nearly spilling out of my dress.

I smiled to myself. I could be Claude's weakness. I could be the woman that could turn his evil thoughts around. I could be the right kind of temptation to make him so very weak.

He continued to pull my head back so he could kiss near my ear. He peered down at me and he could see my nipples hardening by the second. I moaned at the feel of his lips. I moved my hands to feel his dick. He was hard. He was sexy. He was rough. Claude. I could predict that his sex would be that damn good. I gasped as he slid his hand up to cup my breasts.

I moaned, "Claude...please...stop..."

He whispered, "You don't really want me to stop."

He was tempting me, but, I felt a chill again and the hairs on the back of my neck were standing straight up. Before he could blink, I left in a flash. I had to get out of his reach before his power took over and I ended up doing something I would regret.

CHAPTER 5

ESSENCE

I peered through the thick curtains and rubbed what looked like frost on the inside of the bedroom window first thing in the morning. Even though I couldn't take a walk outside, I didn't miss a single sunrise. I watched from behind the glass with envious eyes. The morning had been cold and I was the only one, other than Rain, that had been awake. I was wrapped up in a red robe and it was blissfully warm. That was the closest I would get to feel my own skin warm again.

I missed going to the boulangerie in the mornings to get croissants and a latte when I was human. I still made myself a cup of hot coffee or tea, and although it made me feel warm inside, it didn't last very long. It sometimes made me feel sadder.

I looked over to my right and noticed a small pink wrapped gift on the dresser. I smiled as I went over to it. Where did this come from? It was a gift from my husband. I untied the big bow that had decorated it. I opened the box and slipped out the necklace, earrings, and bracelet made of beautiful jewels. I slid my finger through the ring, admiring the vivid red of the rubies. Rubies reminded me of my foster mother, Joanne. She was good to me while I was in her care. Though I had only been with her for a short time of my teenage life, it was some of the best memories I ever had. I'd spent my childhood going in and out of foster homes in San Francisco. I had been an orphan, abandoned by folks I had never seen before. I'd spent the most time with Joanne. Though she was a white woman and I was black, she never treated me as if we weren't the same.

Memories of her cascaded down like an unexpected rainstorm.

Joanne came in our front door, cursing at the door as usual because the lock always got stuck when she tried to unlock it. It really needed to be replaced. She put a bag of croissants and a few baguettes on the table. She always liked to have bread for breakfast and some later for dinner. Warm croissants were my favorite breakfast treat.

Joanne was a French woman, born and raised in a small town called Brantôme, who had moved to San Francisco with her family as a teenager. She was the reason why I wanted to study abroad in France. She encouraged me to travel and visit her birthplace. No one had ever instilled culture in me. Joanne's culture was the closest I had. I was more than excited about going to Paris. Not to mention, she had spent all her hard-earned money to send me.

"Bonjour Essence, ça va cherie?"

"Oui, ça va," I replied. "I made us some coffee."

She taught me French and I picked it quickly before studying it on my own. She got out the butter dish and a jar of strawberry jam while I put the plates on the table. She helped herself to the coffee and put a croissant on her plate. I grabbed a croissant, sat at the table, and pulled the bread into a few pieces before loading it with creamy white butter and strawberry jam.

Joanne watched me in amusement. She thought it spoiled a good croissant when I put a large glob of butter and jam on it. She always ate hers without anything on it. She sat down at the table and poured creamer and a few tablespoons of sugar into her cup.

"Are you looking forward to studying abroad?" she asked.

"Yeah," I mumbled through the croissant. "I was wondering if we could practice more French before I leave."

"*Ah, oui…*"

I licked my fingers before getting up to pour myself some coffee. I liked to drink mine with hazelnut creamer. "I'm so nervous about it all. I hope I make friends."

"You are a lovely girl. I'm sure you'll make lots of new friends."

I sat back down at the table to finish my breakfast. "I'm sure I will…"

"Hurry and finish. Sitting around in your pajamas at this time of the morning isn't pleasant. You've been up for hours. You should've been showered and dressed before coming to the table for breakfast."

I groaned at her scolding. It was summer vacation. I had graduated from high school. I didn't see a need to be showered and dressed so early, but I answered, "Oh all right. I won't come to the table anymore before bathing."

As soon as I finished my coffee and croissant, I went into the bathroom to wash up. Clouds of steam immediately fogged up the tiny bathroom as the hot water hit the cold air. I washed up in the shower in a speedy manner. I turned off the water and dried off. I put on my underwear, my jeans, and then my T-shirt.

The memory faded as I smiled at the jewels Rain had given me. I adored his gifts. I nearly wished I could go back to how I used to be. At least, I would be able to enjoy the simple pleasures of eating a warm croissant in the morning instead of the bitter-tasting blood I needed to survive. Being a vampire hadn't been entirely evil. Now, I was one of the most beautiful creatures they had ever seen. My transformation had made me more womanly and more stunning. It was nice to be looked at that way.

I wished I could see Joanne's face one more time and see how she was doing. I wrote her letters to tell her I was okay, but I'd sent it in an envelope without an address. I described how beautiful Paris was and how much fun I had been having. She didn't need to know the truth. What I had become would be unbelievable and horrifying.

I put the jewels back into the box and left our bedroom. Rain was in the study, engrossed in a massive old book, which I had seen propped up on display every day. He seemed to find that book very interesting. I never questioned him about what was in it. He never shared what was in it, so I left him alone. He waved absently at me, without taking his eyes off the page. I went over to the window to look out at the morning sun. Tears came to my eyes. I didn't dare wipe them away. I let them fall.

I felt him wrap his arms around my waist as he crept up behind me. He moved his hands up toward the back of my neck. He moved my long hair to the side and placed a kiss on my neck. I felt his hands touch the necklace with the medallion that he had given me. He was removing it from my neck.

"Why are you taking it off?" I asked with a deep frown.

"I'm going to put your necklace in a very safe place. We have a visitor coming when Legend returns," he said. "I don't know if I can trust her yet."

I didn't ask him any questions as he put it into his jacket's pocket. When I faced him, I saw that he had already removed his. He saw the tears in my eyes and wiped them away with his thumb.

"Your memories are getting to you again?"

I nodded slowly. "I miss the little things like being able to walk outside and croissants with warm butter and jelly."

He embraced me and held me close until my sadness faded away. It was always a temporary fix. The sadness would always return tomorrow when the sun came up again.

CHAPTER 6

ULYSSES

Finally, after combing the city for a couple of days, I found the beautiful woman Rain had kicked out of my private party. She was at the park, sitting on a bench, reading a book as the sun hit her perfectly. I loved that I could walk in the day without being burned. I wished all vampires could experience it. It allowed me to be able to see the mortals in natural lighting. The warmth of their blood combined with the sun gave them life. I wondered what I would look like as a mortal. The thought crossed my mind lots of times.

The great thing about sneaking out of Château and going into Paris was that no humans believed vampires were real. We were a myth. Humans came to the Red Light District when their curiosity got the best of them and found out that we weren't a myth. We were very much real and we could give them the best orgasms of their lives. By then, it would be too late. We would nibble at their necks and the pinch they would feel as we drank from them made that silly little myth a reality. Before they could leave, their memories would be wiped clean, and it would all seem like a real dream.

The Covenant forbid for any vampire to travel into Paris. Rain kept that rule enforced, but I didn't care about any rules. I was going to have *her*.

"Hello," I greeted.

She stared at me as if I were a stranger. She didn't recognize me.

How would she, especially if Rain made her forget everything on her way out of the door?

"Hello," she responded. "Enjoying the day?"

"I am now... What are you reading?"

"Some classic literature...*Pride and Prejudice*." She laughed casually.

"Ah, yes, my mother loves that book."

She smiled warmly. "Have a seat."

I sat next to her. "Thank you. It's a beautiful day."

"Yes, it is... My name is Nicole."

"Nice to meet you, Nicole. My name is Ulysses."

Next thing, we were talking and laughing at one another's jokes and I heavily flirted. The time seemed to fly by with a simple conversation. I didn't want to leave her presence so quickly and she didn't appear to mind that I was taking up most of her afternoon. I wanted to prolong this for as long as I could.

"Have dinner with me," I said.

"I would love to join you, but..."

"But what?"

"I'm not dressed to go have dinner right now." She smiled. "I would have to go home."

I chuckled. "I'll go with you, so you can change."

"Sounds like a plan," she replied.

We hopped into a cab and stopped by her place before dinner. I waited outside until she was ready to go. When she invited me in, I declined politely. I proved that I was a gentleman and that she could trust me. I wanted her to believe that.

When she came outside, she looked stunning in a casual cerulean-blue dress. It was perfect for the evening. She didn't take too long to get dressed either.

I didn't know much about places in Paris and she had a small restaurant in mind. I let her order whatever she liked. I ordered food so she wouldn't have to eat alone. I nibbled a little bit of steak but couldn't eat the whole meal. It didn't taste exquisite, but I wasn't worried about the food. Nicole was quite the exciting and sexy distraction. She seemed to be as beautiful as the night before. I could practically taste her sweetness from where I was sitting.

What would it be like to taste her? I wondered. I had to stifle my urge because, for some reason, I felt like making love to her. Something in me felt so strange. I didn't want to lie to her about what I really was and that was rare. I usually didn't care if mortals knew anything about me.

I enjoyed watching her laugh as her eyes sparkled. She was lean, yet curvaceous, and she was wearing the hell out of that dress.

The scent of her was driving me wild while I watched her eat. I craved her. It was as if I needed her blood. I needed her sex. It didn't matter which came first. On any other night, I would've sucked and then fucked her by now, but I was growing tired of meaningless sex. I considered sucking her blood to quench my thirst, but that would do nothing for the erection I felt pressing up against my zipper.

"What's your name, again?" she asked as if she had forgotten that fast.

"Ulysses."

Nicole smiled a little and winked at me. "I have a tiny confession."

"What is it?"

"I'm sorry, but I've been playing a little game with you."

"A game? What kind of game?"

"I knew who you were the moment you walked up to me. I'm fully aware of who and…*what* you are."

She surprised me. I was speechless. She wasn't supposed to remember. Rain always made sure they wouldn't remember. *Why didn't it work on her?* As if she could read my mind, she flashed me a necklace she was wearing.

Observing my confused stare, she replied, "I used a little magic to create this lovely little necklace. It prevents *your kind* from fucking with my mind."

I sat back and observed her little trinket. "My *kind?*"

"Yes, you know what you are." She stared into my eyes with a serious expression.

"Hmmm…so you practice magic?" I asked, switching the subject.

She went along with me brushing over the fact that she knew what I was. "I practice many forms of magic… Does that scare you?"

I never heard about people doing witchcraft against vampires. It didn't seem as if she wanted to use her black magic against me, so I wasn't afraid of her little trinket.

"Nothing scares me, sweetheart."

"I'm sure it doesn't. It isn't a scare tactic. I want you to know that I'm only having dinner because I want to have dinner with you. Your charm and mind hypnosis doesn't work on me."

"Well, that's a first, yet that's good to know. I like it better that you're here with me at your free will."

She smiled. I noticed the way she was clutching her necklace. It was as if she were a Catholic woman holding her Rosary beads.

"I've never seen a vampire that can walk around in the daytime, so I was actually shocked to watch you approach me at the park in broad daylight. Are there others like you?"

I thought of lying and denying what she was claiming, but something made me confirm her accusations. I wanted to see where this would go.

"My uncle and I are the only two that can."

She nodded as her eyes glimmered with fascination. "Hmmm… You're sooooo fine, much like the other men in your family."

I chuckled and raised my eyebrow at her. "Thank you."

"I'm serious. I can stare at you all day."

"Hmmm...is that right?"

"Yes."

"Now that we are done with dinner, what's next?"

Biting on her lower lip, a naughty smile graced her face. "I want you to come home with me."

She had officially turned this date up another notch. I had no idea how deep her black magic was, but I wanted to feel how wet her pussy was. My body was burning, demanding immediate gratification. The burning desire to take her in that restaurant was strong and I couldn't ignore it any longer.

If she did have evil intentions, I was willing to take the risk.

I went with her to her place after I paid for dinner. Once there, I looked around at all the books of spells and talismans she had laid around everywhere. Her desk, her couch, and all her shelves, were filled with piles of books that contained thousands of spells. I wondered how many of them she had read and if she practiced any.

I raised both eyebrows with curiosity. "So, you're a witch... Nice. I've never met a witch before."

"I'm not a witch. I like to think of myself as an Enchantress. I'm still in the learning process, so I don't know very much. But, as you can see, I do a lot of reading."

"Ah, you're a woman who is studying to perform magic to put someone underneath your spell, right?"

"I wouldn't say that. One day, I plan on being magnificent at it."

"What made you want to get into spells?"

"Well, there are a lot of vampires in the Red Light District. I use my necklace to hang out there and I pretended to be under hypnosis so I can come home with the memory of everything I've seen. Gratefully, I've never been bitten...."

I cut her off. "You're lucky you're still alive with all that's going on in the Red Light District these days. It's not safe for a woman as beautiful as you are."

"Luck has nothing to do with it. My necklace works."

I wasn't a believer in her little lucky charm. If a vampire wanted to truly get to her, that necklace wouldn't be a factor. "What are you looking to gain from knowing that vampires are real?"

"I'm deeply fascinated by your kind. The vampires in the Red Light District aren't monsters seeking to terrorize lives violently night after night. I find that vampires are in need of understanding, love, and compassion."

"So you want to be like a vampire social worker or something?"

She laughed at my humor. I was joking and she got my corny joke.

"No, I simply want to draw from a vampire with hundreds of years of sexual experience. Vampires seek to find a perfect lover— to love only her, want only her, and to need only her. He tries to find that one person who can save him from an isolated, miserable and dull eternity of loneliness."

"Seems like you have it all figured out," I replied.

"I want to know more. When I was invited to Pigalle Palace to be your entertainment, I was captivated. I figured the only way to protect myself from being attacked or killed was to wear my necklace and it worked. I plan on making more necklaces and learning more spells so others like me will be able to coexist with vampires without having our memories washed away."

I was curious to learn more about her intentions. "Other than the necklace you wear, have you performed any spells on me?"

"No, I don't have to because you're not threatening to hurt me. The only magic I've used was to protect myself from being manipulated by your kind."

My dick was hard and feeling so heavy in my pants. She sounded sexy as fuck. I had contained myself all evening. I hardly burned this way for another woman—ever. I was becoming obsessed with her, that quickly. *Had she really put a spell on me? Would she tell me if she had?* I wasn't feeling like myself so it had to be magic.

She paid close attention to the way I invaded her personal space.

I could see her own desire in her eyes as I asked, "What do you want to do, now?"

She pulled me close and wrapped her arms around my neck. I bent down to place a kiss on her lips. The touch of her mouth on mine drove me wilder. Her tongue teased the seam of my lips and I opened up for her. I ran my hands through her hair silky feeling. I held her as if she was my precious possession, branding her lips with mine.

My hands moved over her body, leaving a trail of fire wherever I touched. She was moaning. I lifted her off her feet while leaving my mouth on hers. I carried her to her bedroom and lowered her gently onto her bed.

As soon as her back touched her feather down comforter, I removed the articles of her clothing, one by one. I removed that little necklace from around her neck without her knowing. I was that smooth. No magic spell was going to stop me because I wanted her to be under my complete control. She was now vulnerable as I stared down at her intensely. I wanted her to see me, feel me, and to know I couldn't be suppressed by anyone or anything.

"Ulysses," she whispered against my lips.

"Yes?" My hands made their way to her bare breast. I traced her nipple with my fingertips, teasing her.

Her back arched as she uttered, "Ulysses... I..."

"Shh... Don't think about anything else, Nicole. Feel me. Enjoy me."

My mouth covered hers once more. I teased her other nipple as well until it was hard. My fingers made patterns in a circular motion down to her stomach next.

"This must be what it feels like to be under hypnosis," she gasped as she felt for her necklace.

Her eyes widened when she noticed it was gone. Her whole body tensed up and became stiff. I stared into her eyes and she was caught up in the fiery color of them. She was unable to panic any longer. She relaxed.

I chuckled because I was having fun with her. My fingers lowered and I started stroking the softest spot between her thighs. I felt her breath nearly leave her as she gasped.

I commanded, "Spread those legs…wider…"

She did what she was told immediately. She was enjoying how demanding I was. I stroked her pussy through her wetness and it was so slick that my fingers slid inside of her. Nicole moaned and moved her hips to meet my fingers. By the way her hips were gyrating, she wanted more. I pushed my fingers deeper, making slow circles on her most sensitive spot. As I glided my fingers, she moaned louder.

"Ulysses!" she cried in desperation. She was squirming beneath me.

I felt her empty canal and her tight walls clench me. "You're so tight and so wet."

She shuddered while I made her moan louder and louder until I became too much. Breathing hard and fast myself, I kept teasing her clit with my fingers. My pace increased as my thumb stroked her clit simultaneously. She was feeling the demands I was putting on her body by a calculated wiggle of my finger. I wanted her to orgasm as she climaxed and I wanted her to do it right at that very moment.

Suddenly, her release hit hard and fast as her body went into mild spasms. Her juicy pussy lips clenched around my fingers as wetness oozed down my hand.

She kissed me deeply, breathing against my mouth. "Your fingers..."

"What about my fingers?"

"They feel so good."

I removed my lips from hers and kissed along her neck. I licked along the pulsating vein I intended to pierce. My fangs sank into her neck as wave after wave of pleasure took hold of her body. I drank from her, filling her with erotic pleasure, heightening her orgasm to an almost painful intensity.

I continued to drink from her. The taste of her was like an aphrodisiac, flooding me with more sensations that were erotic. She was so intoxicating. I released her when I had enough and I ran my finger over her punctured skin.

She lay in my arms, breathless. I lifted one of her hands and kissed the palm while her other hand slipped down to my jeans, stroking my erection. She felt my size, and the hardness of my shaft; she moaned. Nicole gasped again as my mouth took hers as I tried to devour her. Our kisses were scorching hot and we had this raw need for one another. My tongue swept into her mouth.

Running over her breasts possessively and roughly, my fingers pinched her nipples, sending a shock of waves through her. I took my mouth away from hers once again and threw them back to her breasts and my fingers were right back in her moist heat. She loved the way my strong fingers invaded her.

"You're so wet for me," I said.

"Yes. I want you to fuck me."

"You're not ready for that...yet."

Nicole whimpered a little bit while I went down and buried my head between her thighs. I needed to conquer her pussy with my tongue. My tongue moved along the wet folds in one long lick.

My tongue then spiraled against her clit and she moaned to the heavens. Her pearl tongue was so swollen and so needy. It was begging me to suck her.

As Nicole arched her back, reaching for my mouth with her hips, I took total possession and my tongue sent her over the edge. She was panting more and more in such an erotic pleasure that I wasn't worried about anything else except for getting her to orgasm.

I lapped and nipped at her until she was completely wild and lost, helpless to do anything else but take fistfulls of the covers. She came with a loud cry that burst from her involuntarily. I licked up the cream that had erupted from her and she tasted divine.

I slid her body up and took off my clothes. Once I was naked, I covered her body with mine. I kissed her and slid my hand down to grasp my dick. I brought the head between her legs, pushing my engorged flesh against her hot and wet opening.

"Fuck me now!" she shouted.

As I entered her, I sank back into her neck where I already punctured her. I sucked her blood some more. She tasted too good. I didn't suck her dry and I didn't release my venom. I didn't want to change her and I wasn't going to kill her. I only wanted to satisfy her curiosity about being fucked the Ulysses way.

My erotic bite made her breathing erratic as if it stimulated her. She liked the way my teeth sank into her soft skin. I slid into her, in and out, slowly. She submitted her body to me as if she were ready for anything I had to give. I read her mind clearly and every thought she had passed through me. She was a little scared of how much she was giving me. She didn't have to worry about a thing. I was harmless. Her walls were gripping me as I fucked her. The feel of her was extraordinary. We moaned together while my thrusts became harder and deeper.

She climaxed and she was able to take my rough passion as I

placed her leg on my shoulder. I gave her the best of me until we both came. She touched her neck to see that I actually had bitten her once her trance had worn off. This wasn't a dream. She seemed calm but worried all at the same time as her eyes scanned mine.

"Does this mean I'm going to become a vampire?" She panicked.

"No." I picked up her necklace from the side of the bed and dangled it in front of her eyes. "As long as you're with me, you have no need for this. I didn't hurt you, did I? I merely gave you the pleasure you were seeking."

She gently took the necklace out of my hands and held it in her hand tightly. As she closed her eyes, she snuggled up against me. "Thank you for not hurting me."

"Look at me." I moved her chin up with my two fingers so her eyes could meet mine. "I'll never hurt you. I promise."

She snuggled up closer. "I trust you."

That sounded like music to my ears. The beautiful mortal trusted me.

CHAPTER 7

LEGEND

I found myself traveling along many narrow side streets that eventually led me to a maze of colorful alleys. Blue, red, orange, yellow, and green houses, in no particular order, gave the place character. I had searched nearly every nook and cranny of the Caribbean islands for the female Prototype called Mirage. I wasn't sure if I was finally in the right place. After a few nights of looking all over St. Maarten, Dominica, Guadeloupe, Martinique, and Anguilla, a fervent pull led me to Antigua. I didn't have a system or a traveling plan. It felt like I was going in circles and I hadn't covered all of the Caribbean yet.

I chose one of the narrow winding alleys of Antigua to continue my search. This place must've been where most people feared to walk alone at night; there wasn't a single person in sight. I already had my drink of blood from one of the few thermoses I carried with me so my thirst wouldn't get the best of me, but I was running low. I needed my full strength to be able to tap into Mirage and I was hoping this would be where I would find her.

As I walked, it seemed as if everyone, human or not, had already fled as I stalked in the complete darkness. The shimmer of the moon was the only light I had to see, but my night vision worked fine without it. I carefully headed down the cobbled street lined with bi-level, textured, multicolored houses with thick walls and columns along both sides of the narrow alley. As torn sheets blew in the broken windows from the wind, I wondered where everyone was. It was as if the people who lived there could sense, beforehand, that I was coming. They were hiding from me or maybe they were afraid of someone else.

I was set on finding Mirage no matter what.

As if she could read my mind, I heard her say, *"Legend, you're here."*

I halted because her voice was so clear and seemed as if she were right in front of me. My heart beat a little faster. I felt a sudden rush of adrenaline; I was in the right place.

"Where are you?"

I felt something pulling me in her direction as if there was some invisible magnetic force leading me.

"I'm far too weak to keep this up… Please hurry. You don't have much time."

"Keep talking to me," I ordered as I moved up the alley, following her psychic trail.

"Hurry…"

"I'm doing my best…" I was anxious and ready to come face to face. I was drawing very near to her spirit. Though she was weak, our connection was growing stronger by the second. I continued to travel faster than a human eye could detect, trying to zero in on her exact location. "Hold tight."

"I'm afraid."

"Afraid of what?"

Straight ahead, farther down the long alley, was another abandoned white house with a perfectly painted blue door. It was the largest out of all the others and the tallest, at three levels high. I had a feeling that this might've been where she was. I went to one of the broken windows of the house, finding that our connection was the strongest it had ever been. As soon as I stepped foot into the house, I braced myself. It was like someone was breathing on the back of my neck. I turned around, but no one was there.

Caked-up dust covered all the shelves and nothing seemed to have been touched for years. I walked through a few cobwebs as I made my way to the staircase. I swatted them away and looked up the stairs. The house was too quiet. I tried to listen for any movement, but the only thing I could hear were rats running on the floors to hide and the sound of my footsteps going up the noisy, creaking staircase.

As soon as I went into what seemed to be the master bedroom, my breathing became dense. In the bed was a body, but I couldn't tell if that's what it really was, so I got closer.

I went to the bedside, looking down to get the first glimpse of whoever it was in the bed. My heart started beating in a wild rhythm as soon as I saw her dark-brown hair sprawled out on the pillow underneath her. She looked so delicate and fragile. She was indeed dying. When she fluttered her eyelashes to stare up at me, the dark circles around her eyes and her wrinkled skin let me know that she hadn't had blood in a very long time. She looked like a breathing corpse.

Touching her temple lightly, I couldn't feel her energy. She was moments from passing away. I had come in time.

I took out a thermos full of blood, took the top off, and put it up to her lips. She tightly kept her lips pursed together.

Through our telepathic connection, she said, *"I need your blood. Only your blood will save me."* Her mouth didn't move as she spoke to me. She was still using her mind to communicate.

Why did she need my blood? Was this some sort of setup?

Then, it dawned on me about what Azura had said before I left. I should've known better. She was a Prototype. She didn't need average human blood to be revived. She needed *royal* vampire blood. The thought of her draining me dry came to mind, but for some reason, I trusted her. Without thinking twice, I held my wrist up to her mouth. She was far too weak to bite me, so I had to bite my own wrist. Blood oozed from me as I held it up to her mouth.

While she drank, the wrinkles in her skin started going away instantly. As she regained strength, she drank faster. I stroked her hair with my free hand.

"My brother Rain's blood would've healed you quicker."

She exhaled as she removed my wrist from her mouth. As if coming up from underwater, she took a deep breath. "His blood is too powerful. His blood can kill me."

I held the open gash as it healed before my eyes. "How'd you end up like this?"

"An order for a hex was cast upon me… It's a long story."

"You had a little trouble with a Spellbinder?"

"Yes…I'd been in hiding for a full century now. A few months ago, a Spellbinder found me. I didn't think of her as a threat, but she must've thought I was. I went to bed and woke up to find that I couldn't move. It was nothing you can imagine. Now, I have to see if the spell has been broken." She sat up and moved one leg over the edge of the bed. She smiled happily. "It's all over with now. You saved me. Thank you, Legend."

"You're welcome, Mirage."

"Please call me MiMi."

"Okay, MiMi."

I couldn't help but notice that MiMi wasn't just beautiful as her blue skin transformed into a light-golden brown before me. She was gorgeous. Her eyes were the color of lavender, much like the color of the lavender fields of France. I had never seen anyone of our kind with purple eyes, but they went beautifully with her creamy-looking, hazelnut-colored skin.

"I need to get back to Paris. It's not safe here… I'm not sure how many Spellbinders are here. Usually when there's one, there are a few others."

"I'll take you back to Paris with me. The King needs to speak with you anyway."

"The King? Well, that sounds like music to my ears. He knows that I'm alive?"

"Yes, he does."

She smiled widely. "At last, he has taken his seat on the throne. It's been a long time coming."

"Yes, Rain has finally accepted his birthright," I replied proudly. "Our nephew, Ulysses, has grown into a man before our eyes. He's also been given the title of the Divine One, so I guess you can say that we have a Divine Duo. He's a Pureblood, born to my brother, Onyx, and his wife, Soleil."

Her ears perked up as her smile faded. She hadn't known about Ulysses and seemed very interested. "A Pureblood?"

"Yes."

"If he's Pureblood, then it isn't possible for Rain to be the King. There can only be one Divine One, according to the Divination... one King." She paused when she realized that she was saying something that we hadn't taken into consideration. She quickly changed the subject, "You must take me back to Paris. I must meet both of them. What is the young prince doing to prepare himself?"

"Other than lying with countless mortals, night after night, he's not doing much of anything."

"I see...King Rain takes care of everything?"

"Yes."

"That shall soon change."

I frowned, trying to figure out what she was trying to imply. Was Ulysses supposed to be King while Rain was still living? What was the real reason for me coming to the Caribbean?

"Why'd you call me here?"

"There are a lot of things that you won't understand yet. It isn't time for you to know it all, but one of the reasons I called you here is because... you are to be my husband."

I nearly choked on my own saliva. "Wait... What?"

"You're Legend, aren't you? The firstborn son of Valerie?"

I nodded. I had never heard the name Valerie before. Was that my mother's name?

She continued, "You are to be my mate, my true love, my better half, and keeper of my soul. It has been arranged before you were born. I can only marry one from Allemand and Christione's line. I've waited for this day."

"My mother's name was Valerie?"

I had no memory of her. Rain had been so lucky. He was given the opportunity to remember everything about her, including the way she looked. The rest of us could remember nothing about her.

"Yes... Her name was Valerie. You didn't know that?"

"No. Look, I don't understand all of this..." I ran my hand over my long dreads and sighed.

Everything she was telling me was so confusing. I really didn't understand why she needed me. She was much older and much stronger than I could ever be. I wasn't a weak man, but I wasn't so sure about being the man she wanted me to be. She was speaking about something that seemed to be prearranged. *Was this my destiny?*

"Rain's destiny was to save us from the Préfet and marry whom he has chosen. If another Pureblood prediction had been mentioned, you and your siblings would've never managed to escape with Selene and Mortimer. Where are they now? Are they in the Palace?"

I had never heard my godparents' real names either.

"No, Rain banned them from the Kingdom for his reasons."

"I see," she said with her voice dropping in disappointment. She had paused for a moment before she said, "You know that you were never meant to marry that horrible mortal...right?"

Chantal wasn't meant for me, but how did Mirage know any of this? If she was kept here in the Caribbean under some type of magic, how in the world did she know all of this?

As if she could read my thoughts and me, she eased out of the bed and stood in front of me. My blood was running through her and she had transformed from the corpse that had been lying there dying into a perfect-looking young goddess.

"Do not be afraid of me, Legend. It's okay not to have all of the answers. It's also okay to be leery, but I want you to trust me. Wouldn't you like to spend the rest of your eternity with me?"

MiMi made me quiver on the inside, far before I came face to face with her. She was the most beautiful, compelling woman I had ever met. From the moment she subconsciously contacted me, I was drawn like a moth to an open flame.

She reached for me and eased into my arms. Suddenly, I felt a jolt of energy surge throughout my entire body. The slightest touch from her was electrifying. I was completely consumed by MiMi's power. As her lips touched mine, her hands ran over my dreads.

I swallowed hard and said, "Let's get out of here. I have to get you to the Château."

With her hand in mine, we fled.

CHAPTER 8

AZURA

I felt suddenly depressed over the next few days. Ever since I had come back from the club, I hadn't been feeling like being cooped up in the Château moping around. There wasn't shit else to do. Club Vaisseau was calling me to come back or maybe it was Claude calling me to come back. Whichever one, I wanted to run back and quickly. I had fight within myself. Nothing good could come out of me going back there, but I'd had so much fun. The Château was so boring.

I went over to the window and looked out while naked. I had gotten out of the bathtub. I was going to have to find a new hobby. I had nothing to do since I was no longer opening up the club every night. After doing it for so long, I couldn't get used to not going down there. I felt almost back to normal when I went down there the other night. Life in the Château was so blah. I didn't want to do Princess stuff with Queen Essence and I definitely wasn't interested in hearing Rain rant repeatedly about everything that wasn't going right. It wasn't like he was doing shit about it.

I made up my mind. I was going to go back. I was going to have a great time. I was going to avoid Claude.

I showered, slipped into a red dress and pumps. I didn't bother drying my hair. I let it look wild and curly. My thoughts had been scattered ever since running away from Claude.

It was as if I wanted to see him again; like had no other choice. Something was drawing me to him.

I felt the sexual tension between us on that dance floor. I wanted desperately to forget my lustful thoughts about Claude because I didn't believe in love at first sight at all. I considered lust at first sight, most definitely. Lust was supposed to be something that I could control and something that I could redirect down another path. When it came to Claude, I was losing my self-control. This had never happened to me.

I headed to Club Vaisseau as soon as I was dressed.

Claude was leaning up against the bar as soon as I entered through the front doors. He was talking to a curvy, chocolate-skinned mortal with a voluptuous ass. She was wearing a catsuit and it showed off all her assets. She was working the hell out of that outfit. She was flirting with him and flipping her hair. She was quite delicious-looking. Jealousy filled me for a split-second as I had thoughts of sucking her blood until she became lifeless, but then it went away.

I wasn't going to worry about her. Shit, she could join us if she wanted. All thoughts I had about ignoring him went out of the window. Claude couldn't take his eyes off me as soon as I walked past him. I made up my mind the moment we locked eyes that I wasn't going to go to him. I was going to make him come to me. I floated across the dance floor, taking in the stares from all the other men that wanted me, too. Sexy mama in the catsuit was doing her thing and I was watching her.

Liquor, sweat, blood, and sex were all around me and I didn't mind it. Their energy turned me on. I was starting to enjoy what was going on in that club. It was better than sitting in the Château with nothing else to do.

Claude couldn't stop staring at me. I could feel his eyes penetrating through me. He wasn't going to let me walk up in his club and stroll on by him as if I hadn't seen him. That was a no-no in his eyes. Without warning, he was upon me, with his hand on my arm roughly.

He pulled me against his body and said with his lips grazing my ear, "Don't tell me you came here to dance without me."

I trembled in his arms. He felt it because a slight smirk graced his face. I replied, "You seem to know what I want, so you tell me what I came here to do."

With those words, he took me up the spiral staircase. There would be no running away from him this time; I didn't want to run. I wanted to see what was going to happen next between us. He took me to one of the biggest private soundproof rooms.

Immediately, he leaned down and kissed my shoulder. I moaned and allowed him to put his hand around my throat. Instead of choking me, he kissed me tenderly. He eased the straps of my dress down. The dress fell to my feet, exposing my naked body. He reached around and cupped my breasts. His hands were full as he took my nipples between his forefinger and thumb. He squeezed.

Claude turned me around roughly and pressed his lips to mine. As our mouths opened up for one another, our tongues danced. Palming my ass, I was at his mercy. Soon, his fingers were exploring the folds of my pussy and I rocked against his hand to show him that I didn't wear any panties in case something like this happened.

A look of pleasure took over Claude's stern face and as his finger explored me, I moaned. Suddenly, Rain's face flashed behind my closed lids and it startled me. Rain was using his power.

Fuck! He knew where I was and whom I was with.

"Stop," I muttered against his lips, trying to pull away.

He pulled me back toward him. "I won't stop, Azura. Forget that I'm the leader of the Ravens. Forget about Rain. Forget about Pigalle Palace. I'm on fire for you. I want you. Azura, you're what I *need*. Don't you need me?"

With each word, I melted in his arms. "Don't stop..."

I unbuckled his pants and he turned me over, pushed me up against the wall. When he entered me, my whole body submitted entirely. He fucked me deep and hard. I screamed to the heavens. He felt as good as I thought he would. Something about Claude had me hypnotized and I almost felt as if I were summoned to him. He made me want to belong to him for eternity.

As soon as our hot steamy sex was over, I attempted to dress quickly.

"Not so fast," he said, beating me to the door before I could walk away so quickly. "You can't walk up in here, fuck me, and then leave me."

I snapped at him, "I can do whatever I want."

He chuckled. "I don't operate that way, sweetheart. Stay a little while. I want to introduce you to the Ravens."

"I'm not going anywhere near those rogues."

"What are you afraid of? They won't harm you."

"Look, don't take this personally, but I will never hang out with your minions. They are out of control. You'd better get them in line before..."

"Before what?" He smirked. "I'm not afraid of you or your siblings. King Rain can try to enforce the stupid rules all he wants. I don't give a shit. You know you want to see what real freedom tastes like. Come and join us, Azura. We would love to have you."

I must've been under Claude's spell because I didn't protest any further. I was off to meet the Ravens.

CHAPTER 9

AZURA

It was dark inside the room except for a group of candles in each corner. This room was one that I used to know all too well. I'd had plenty of threesomes and orgies in here. It looked entirely different with the red velvet walls and black carpet making the room seem darker. The brood was talking and laughing amongst them. I counted about fifteen bodies; all who appeared to become silent, once they realized Claude wasn't alone.

"I want you all to meet Azura," Claude announced.

"*Princess* Azura," I corrected.

"Excuse me…Princess Azura," Claude said with a smile.

I felt their eyes. They didn't speak as they stared.

To fill the silence, Claude said, "She is a friend of mine and she is welcome here."

The brood went right back to talking, but now their eyes were piercing through me. No matter what Claude said, I wasn't welcomed and they didn't care what title he gave me. I wasn't to be trusted.

Claude took my hand and led me over to the next room. It was once my godparents' office, but it was now what looked like his bedroom. Instantly, I wished I wasn't there anymore. *What was I getting myself into?* Claude's eyes were filled with lust. I wanted him, to be close to him and to feel his dick pressed up against me, but I also wanted to feel safe and content with his presence. I didn't want this to be our last time hooking up, but it was going to be.

His smile was radiant as he smiled down at me. When he laughed, his whole face lit up. He didn't seem like he was the leader of something so dark, something so evil that they were indeed the most feared creatures in all of Paris.

Reading my thoughts, his smile faded. He didn't like what I was thinking. To switch up the mood, he went back to doing what worked best with us, sexual desire. Claude stared down and admired my curve-fitting dress that revealed a tempting amount of cleavage.

"You're so beautiful, Princess Azura. You deserve to have the best things in life... But, not without me..."

"That's so sweet of you... But, let's be real here for a moment: I could never fall in love with a blood-sucking monster like you," I said.

He looked amused at how serious I was being. He took in my features and my natural elegance as he placed both hands gently on my face.

"You have this rare aura of light. I'm so curious. I don't want to hurt you. You're too beautiful and delicate to mistreat."

Something sparked from within me. It was something I hadn't felt in a very long time. No one had ever spoken to me that way. *Was this the feeling Rain spoke of? Was this what love felt like?*

I suddenly became envious of Claude. My new life wasn't the way I wanted it to be. I didn't mean to spend the rest of my eternity in the dull Château, doing whatever Rain told me to do.

"It must be kind of cool to live the way you do. You're able to do what you want and when you want," I uttered.

"If you ever get a chance to live the way I do, you will find that it is the greatest feeling. I'm sure you love living in luxury and having people wait on you hand and foot. But, it feels like a punishment being told what to do and what not to do. Where to go and where not to go... Am I right?"

I was afraid to reply, afraid to reveal that I hated the invisible shackles that seemed to be on each of my ankles, but I didn't have to say a word. I was enticed by the inferior creature before me. He was so ruggedly handsome. He was fighting for a cause that I found to be ruthless and pointless, but I had seen a glimpse of the real in him. That's what had me at that moment. Yet, he intimidated me by the way he stared at me. It was as if he was trying to pierce open my body to see into the very depths of my soul. That scared me.

Suddenly, he snapped his fingers and a mortal was thrown into the room. She fell at his feet with her hands tied in front of her. She was naked, scared and shaking. She cried as he lifted her onto her feet. As he held her body in front of his, he stared at me.

I stared at him, wondering what he was going to do with her.

With his finger, he traced the side of her neck. He grabbed her hair and tilted her back toward him roughly. Without wasting any time, he jammed his sharp fangs against her skin. I could hear the sound of her flesh tearing. He sucked her blood greedily, not caring that he was about to kill her. I watched him as he watched me while drinking her blood. Suddenly, the girl's body went limp and he loosened up his hold on her. He pulled his fangs out and I watched her body fall to the floor with a loud thud.

He wiped his mouth with the back of his hand as he continued to stare at me. His eyes were light-electric blue, almost looked silver as he glared at me.

"I should go," I said quickly, but once again, my attempt of escaping him was cut short.

"Come here." His voice was commanding and profound. He wrapped his arm around my waist. "I didn't give you permission to leave." His words sent shivers down my spine as he continued to stare at me. One of his hands tried to touch my lips, but I cringed back. "I won't hurt you," he promised. "My world can be gorgeous if you let me show it to you."

I froze. I wasn't shocked by his invitation. I was surprised by how quickly things had been happening between us. For some reason, I suddenly felt safe, there with him.

What was he doing to me? What was he doing to my mind?

I moved my eyes from his eyes because they were terrifying me. I was afraid I wouldn't be able to escape him.

"Look at me," he demanded.

He quickly snapped my face toward him so that my eyes were once again on him.

"I would like to get to know you," he continued with a more gentle voice. "You're interesting. I don't find many things interesting, but you...you're intoxicating..." As I was about to refuse him again, he interrupted me, "I'm not a man that takes no for an answer," he warned.

A part of me felt like I was at a crossroad. I felt guilty for being there and I was held liable for flirting with the possibilities of what I could be with the enemy. Claude could sense my loneliness and pain and he was using that against me. It was evident that I really didn't want to leave because I was still there staring into his eyes.

I could picture us making sweet passionate love, but I also could see all the lives he took in a blink of an eye. These two dangerous paths, yet two possibilities, and two entirely different fates could leave me fighting my family.

Without thinking any more about it, I let him take my lips. I was so wrapped up in his kiss that soon we were sprawled out across his bed, giving into every desire imaginable. Claude was taking over my body and it felt so good. I didn't think about the mortal lying dead on the floor either. I only concentrated on the way he was making me feel.

CHAPTER 10

RAIN

Five more bodies had been found dead in the alleys of the Red Light District. It was all over the news. I was beginning to hate watching the news. Every other day another body was added to the count. Speculations were swirling around that they thought wild wolves had attacked them. Humans were funny. Wolves? There were no wild wolves in Paris—only blood-sucking vampires. No person had lived to witness to any vampire accounts, but how long would it be before one slipped through the cracks?

As my confidantes and personal servants delivered more unwanted news about Azura going to Vaisseau behind my back as I suspected, my head swirled with ways to start putting things back in order. I used my telekinetic powers to see that Azura was sleeping with the enemy. The Ravens were filled with so much hate and it made me angry that my own sister had betrayed me, yet again.

Two nights in a row, Azura was drinking, dancing, and in Claude's bed. That had me outraged.

"Has Azura returned yet?" I asked Essence as she entered the living room.

"Not yet. Legend hasn't either," she replied.

I was also awaiting Legend's return so I could see what it was that Mirage indeed wanted. In the meantime, I did a little research in the library.

While reading the book that was encased in glass in the center of the room, I discovered that it traced our family's history back to the Prototypes of Egypt. Alaina and Neve were Allemand's parents, vampires bitten by bats, but they weren't born that way. Syria and Fabian were also vampires that had been bitten by bats, Christione's parents. Evan and Mirage were a brother and sister who had been bitten by bats when they were twenty years old. Unable to deal with their blood thirsts, they had their first feed on their human family. Syria and Fabian took them in so they could be around other vampires. Since Evan and Mirage had no one to marry, it was promised that Evan and Mirage would be able to marry any descendants of Allemand and Christione.

One day, Alaina, Neve, Syria, and Fabian were decapitated and burned to death for creating Purebloods Allemand and Christione. Allemand and Christione fled from Egypt to Paris with Evan and Mirage, in fear that they, too, would be murdered. They found Pigalle Palace and were safe with the vampires of the Red Light District. They were named King and Queen because the Parisian vampires had never seen two Purebloods. Evan and Mirage were the only living Prototypes, so they had a home in the kingdom as well. King Allemand and Queen Christione had one daughter, Valerie, and she was born human. That was something that couldn't be explained and the whole kingdom became outraged.

Valerie was sent far away from the kingdom. She married a vampire and gave birth to four half-breed children, Legend, Azura, Onyx, and me. It was promised that Legend was to marry Mirage, and her brother, Evan, was supposed to marry Azura because they were the first two born.

I had done enough research to know that Mirage was alive and she was to be Legend's wife. Where was Evan if he was supposed to marry Azura? I wondered.

As I read further, I discovered that a Prototype had killed King

Allemand and Queen Christione for giving birth to a human daughter. It was an abomination because the hopes of a growing royal family were high. The same Prototype found my mother and father and killed them, too. They didn't want any half-breed children to rule the palace. We were saved by our godparents and kept safe. The Divination cleared it up that I would come back to rule over Pigalle if I proved to be a Daywalker once transformed.

Which Prototype killed my family if all the others were dead long before that happened? It was either Mirage or Evan who had killed them. They were the only two left in this equation. Mirage was going to have to give me some answers.

Gently, Azura pushed open one of the garden's French double doors as she entered. I looked up from the book and snapped my head in her direction.

She let out a sigh as she carefully closed the door. I could tell immediately that she was aware that I knew everything she had been doing behind my back. Our eyes connected and I could see her guilt that she tried to hide from me. If she had a beating heart, it would've raced and I would've snatched it out of her chest. I had never seen this look from her. It was a look of betrayal and hurt. Her hands looked as if they were trembling with fear, as she stood frozen in place.

"Where have you been?" I asked. My voice was casual but laced with a cold, threatening tone.

Azura faced me entirely. I took a good look at her. She seemed to be terrified of what I was going to do. She wasn't sure how to provide me with a plausible and satisfying answer without giving up the truth. She stood at the far end of the room and leaned against one of the tall windows. The natural moonlight illuminated her figure and cast a long silhouette along the wooden floor. Her face was shadowed, but even by the moon's light, I could tell she was afraid.

"I... I..." Her voice was a broken whisper.

"Don't bother lying. Where were you?"

She pressed her back up against the wall, tempted to dash away, but the logical side of her brain decided against it. Not only could she not outrun me, she didn't have the power to beat me, either. Her whole body started to shake.

There was a long pause.

When Azura wouldn't give me the answer, I dashed across the room to stand before her. I gently used my index finger to brush her flushed cheeks.

"You're hiding something, sister," I said as my fangs emerged.

"I'm...I'm not hiding anything."

"Where were you?"

"I went for a walk in the gardens to clear my mind and I got so caught up in my thoughts, I lost track of time."

I laughed at her and growled, "Lies."

Suddenly, one of my hands roughly took hold of Azura's neck. Out of pure instinct, she began to struggle to get out of my grasp.

"I know where you went and who you were with," I hissed harshly. "You dare play me for a fool?"

I made no effort to hide the rage boiling inside of me as I pressed my body against hers. She needed to be careful of her every action because I had the power to destroy her with the snap of my fingers. She wasn't going to fight fire with fire. That would only make a bigger fire. I pressed my head up against the crook of her neck, inhaled her. I could smell him. *Claude.*

My breath became uneven. "I'm going to tell you this one time and one time only. You're not allowed to touch him ever again! Do you hear me?"

She nodded slowly. Once I eased off her, she fled down the hall.

Tears threatened to appear behind my eyelids. I didn't want to think my own sister would do this to me on purpose. Her sexual desire was trying to get the best of her, but if she wasn't careful, Claude was going to turn her against me. That was something I wasn't going to stand for. Once love entered the playing field, there would be no way she would stand by my side. She would choose her lover.

Essence sighed and rubbed my shoulder. "Azura loves you, Rain."

"I love her, too, but what will happen once she falls in love with Claude?"

"You think she would let that happen?"

"She already has."

Freedom was something the whole household wanted. It was what Ulysses, Legend, and Azura wanted most. They wanted freedom without caring about what would happen if they truly had that freedom. It was my job to protect them and to protect the kingdom. As soon as I got rid of the problem in the Red Light District, I would give them the freedom that they wanted. They were going to have to be patient with me.

CHAPTER 11

LEGEND

I walked into the Château with MiMi. The travel from Antigua seemed to take longer than expected. I had to keep her replenished with plenty of blood and that took a lot of stopping. Since she was depleted, she drank a lot more and needed much more rest. I wound up running out of thermoses, so we had to drink from a few humans. That was something I really didn't want to do, but we made sure we didn't kill them and we wiped their memories clean once we were done.

"Took you long enough..." Rain's words echoed through the corridor.

That was his way of greeting us. His tone made me look at him to see if he was angry with me for taking so long. I couldn't see his emotions because he hid them very well.

MiMi took a good look at Rain and she bowed graciously before him.

Suddenly, Rain took a step forward and went so close to MiMi's body that he was nearly towering over her.

"Rise before your King," he said.

Her head was still slightly bowed and her eyes remained lowered. "Yes, your highness."

"Who are you?" Rain's cold and cruel voice erupted.

I tried to answer for her, but Rain put his hand up to quiet me.

"I said who are you?" Rain repeated himself, but this time his voice was stronger, more in control and more demanding. "Answer your King!"

MiMi lifted her eyes and replied in a calm manner. "My name is Mirage Oleander, your highness, and I'm the only living Prototype."

Rain had paused for a moment before he said, "A Prototype murdered my mother and father... What do you know about it? Were you the one that killed them?" Rain's voice was so icy that it chilled the room.

I never heard about who killed our family, so the fact that Rain was aware of that much surprised me.

"You have so much to learn, your highness... Alaina, Neve, Syria, Fabian, my parents, Princess Valerie, and her husband were all murdered because no one understood why there were Purebloods or why your mother was born human. Instead of dealing with the unexplainable, they got rid of them. I had nothing to do with that..."

"There are only *two* living Prototypes..."

She interrupted him, "There *were*, but as you can see, I'm the last one standing."

"What happened to Evan?" Rain asked intensely.

"My brother..." She paused at the memory of him. "Evan is no longer alive."

"Did your brother murder my family?"

MiMi looked as if she struggled to reply, but she nodded as she confirmed, "Yes...he did, but he was given strict orders to do so."

"Who gave the order?"

MiMi blinked a few times. "You don't know?"

"Don't be coy with me. Who gave the order?"

"Members of the Préfet gave the order. They thought it would work better for vampires if they had an order in place by a government, but as long as there were Prototypes still living, they wouldn't be able to have the power to do it. Once King Allemand brought the Divination forth the day he was murdered, the Préfet knew the kingdom would have to be restored as soon as you grew up. They tried to hunt you down and kill you, but you were somewhere safe. They gave up on finding you, hoping you would never return. Once your family returned to Paris, they kept a good eye out on you. You didn't seem to want to be King. When they heard of the birth of Ulysses, another Pureblood, they had to finally put the Divination to the test."

Rain held his composure, standing tall and upright. I could tell he didn't think the members of the Préfet had their hands in our family's demise.

"How did your brother die?"

"The Préfet burned him."

"Why?"

"They wanted no other Prototypes to be able to live to bring your family back to the throne. Once Evan killed your family, I fled because I was next. The Caribbean seemed to be the safest place, but I was wrong. A Spellbinder cast that damned spell. I'm sure the Préfet had something to do with it."

"Well...it seems like you have all the answers to most of my questions. I'm sure you know all about this royal family. Purebloods can never actually die. They are merely sleeping, waiting to be awakened."

Rain's eyes didn't meet mine because he didn't want to see how angry I was getting from being kept away from so many secrets. I should've known these things.

MiMi smiled and replied, "Yes, they're here and they're not dead. They're sleeping."

"Do you know where?"

"Yes, I do. Do you have the keys?"

Rain stared at her sternly. I was wondering why Rain wasn't answering as quickly as he had before. He and Essence used to wear the keys around their necks. When I looked at his neck, it wasn't hanging there anymore. I frowned. What was going on?

"Do you have the keys? Both of them?" she asked with wide, curious eyes.

Rain took note of how curious she was and refused to answer her. "What brings you back to Pigalle Palace?"

"I came for what is rightfully mine."

"And what is that?" he continued to badger.

"My husband. I'm to be Legend's wife."

She was bold enough to say it to Rain. I was confused every time she said it. If this were true, why didn't I know anything about it? I watched carefully to see Rain's reaction.

"Yes, I'm aware. Evan was supposed to marry Azura?"

"Yes, but he's dead."

I was more confused, but I didn't show it. I felt Rain had too many secrets and I wasn't sure if it was for our protection, but it was frustrating trying to put all the pieces together on my own.

"They hoped that you would be dead, but as I can see, you're not dead and now you want to marry Legend."

"Do I have your blessing to come back to the kingdom?"

"Yes. I'll let you back in the kingdom but only if Legend agrees. If I find out that you have other intentions, I'll have you locked away forever. I will keep you in a dark dungeon and never let you go. You will resent me and wish that you were dead. Having my brother's hand in marriage is an honor and a privilege. Millions of women would kill to have him. Think about that, Mirage."

She nodded. "None of those women would ever work out because this is the way things are supposed to be."

Rain had observed her for a quick second before he turned to me. "Legend?"

"Yes?"

"You want to marry her?"

I swallowed hard. I was being put on the spot and I didn't like it. Sure, she was beautiful and she was sexy, but I didn't know much about her. I wanted to get to know her.

I didn't answer. I stared at the both of them. They were pushing this on me without me having to make the decision. If I said no, MiMi would possibly run off, and if I said yes, then I would've felt forced to do so.

"Show her to her room on the other side of the palace," Rain said before I could say a word. "That's where she will stay until you marry."

I was glad that was over and I didn't have to answer. I almost thought Rain was going to rip her head off anyway if she said the wrong thing. I noticed the way Rain was staring at her and he didn't quite trust her yet. Hell, I wasn't sure if I believed her.

We walked away and headed down one of the corridors.

She looked to breathe easier now that we were away from Rain.

"Can I trust you?" I felt I needed to ask.

"You don't have to worry about me. You can always trust me and so can the family... Where's everyone else? I would love to meet the rest of the royal family, especially your nephew...the Pureblood Prince."

"I'm sure they're around here somewhere. Don't worry. You'll meet all of them soon."

She smiled and it was a heart-melting smile. Her intense lavender-colored eyes made me want to swoon. We walked down to her assigned bedroom.

"This is where you'll be sleeping. There's a bathroom right on the other side of this wall. Let the maids know if they can get you anything that you might need."

"Thank you. When I lived in Pigalle, the Prototypes were given their own homes. It was quite lonely being there without someone to love."

"How did you get through it?"

"I had lovers and some I were quite fond of, but I had to wait for you." Before she entered her bedroom, she said, "Well? You want to come in?"

I walked in with her and she looked around a bit. She took a good look at the furniture. "Things need to be updated a little in here. At least everything has been dusted."

"Rain made sure the Château was spotless before moving in. Every nook and cranny was cleaned well."

She walked up behind me. "Do you want to marry me? It's okay to state how you feel. Arranged marriages are never really fun."

I inhaled and exhaled deeply as I turned to face her. "It's not that I don't want to marry you. I feel so rushed."

"I've waited for you... I've waited for this moment so it doesn't feel rushed to me."

Very gently, with the tip of my finger, I traced the outline of her lips, a touch of a butterfly brushing up against the most beautiful flower. I could feel her shudder underneath me. She looked into my eyes and those beautiful eyes of hers were taking over my own.

"I've never seen eyes like yours," I admitted. "They're so unique."

"My eyes turned this way once I was given the curse of being a vampire..."

She was too beautiful, too gorgeous, and strikingly breathtaking. I had been with many vampires, but none that captivated me as she had. She was really something. I continued to caress the side of her face. She kissed my hand. I brought her body close to mine and I kissed her forehead.

Suddenly, she pushed me to the bed. Her hands caressed my chest up and down as she got on top of me and straddled my waist. She slowly leaned down and kissed the bottom of my jawline seductively. I placed my hands on both sides of her face and brought her up to my lips. I kissed her neck and she moaned. My left hand wrapped around her waist tightly.

Before we could strip off our clothing, Onyx cleared his throat. He was standing in the doorway, staring at us. I eased from up under her quickly. We were saved from bonding too rapidly. I wasn't thinking straight. I nearly let lust push us too fast.

"Looks like I'm interrupting something. I would come back, but this is urgent," Onyx said.

"What's up?"

"Have you seen Ulysses?" he asked with panic in his voice.

"No, I returned about a half hour ago. Why?"

"He's been gone for over twenty-four hours and no one seems to know where he went. I think he might've gone to Paris…again."

"What? What do you mean he's been gone for twenty-four hours?"

"You heard me. He's nowhere in Pigalle Palace—period."

"Why does your son keep going to Paris? What's in Paris? He knows better. Didn't he learn from the last time we caught him over there? It feels like déjà vu all over again. You know he might be pulling that Rain shit. You remember how many times we had to chase him down in Paris while he was chasing Essence?"

Onyx sighed. "Yeah, I remember. He's rebelling right now and it's because Rain keeps ending his orgy parties. Rain wants you to come with me to find him."

I looked over at MiMi. She was sitting in the middle of the bed, staring at the both of us. Onyx stared at her. He cleared his throat to give me the hint that I needed to introduce them.

"Onyx, this is Mirage Oleander. MiMi, this is my brother, Onyx." She waved. "Hello."

Onyx nodded. "Nice to meet you, MiMi. I'm sorry to steal him away, but we have to go find my son before I kill him my damned self."

"It's all right. Family comes first. I'll see you when you all return."

"I'll be back," I said to her.

"All right."

I walked down the corridor with Onyx.

"Ulysses doesn't like being under Rain's rules," Onyx said.

"Shit, it's the same rules that were in place when the Préfet was here. He was born under these rules so why is everyone tripping? We can't be seen wandering around Paris. It's too dangerous," I replied. "The Ravens are taking over."

"That's what I keep telling him."

We rushed out of the Château.

"I'll drive," I said.

We headed to the garage to get one of the cars.

CHAPTER 12

ULYSSES

I sensed something warm against my cold flesh. I wasn't used to waking up to having something warm in the bed next to me, but I think I liked it. Matter of fact, I loved every moment of it. She snuggled up against me and made me feel warmer. Her hands rubbed my back, up and down, and this feeling came over me. What was this? Was this what love felt like?

I wondered if my cold skin felt too cold to her, but she didn't seem to mind as she snuggled closer, placing her face into my chest. I could feel her warm breath as she breathed in and out. I slowly opened my eyes to see Nicole wrapping her arms around me tightly as if she didn't want me to escape from her.

By now, everyone was probably looking for me. I realized how long I had been gone. I wanted to stay awhile longer, but Rain probably wanted my head on a stake.

"What time is it?" I asked her.

She looked at her clock on the nightstand. "It's five thirty."

"In the evening?"

"Yeah."

"I slept that long?"

"Yeah. I got up and had breakfast and lunch without you." She giggled.

"Damn. I should be leaving now," I said.

She groaned, "Noooo."

"I gotta get back home."

Removing her head from my chest, she stared up into my eyes. "I keep forgetting you have royal duties. It must be nice to be a Prince."

"Not really." I eased out of her arms and out of the bed.

While I dressed, she wrapped the white sheet around her body to cover up. She observed me with a naughty grin on her face. A part of me wanted to wrestle her and pin her down on that bed, but that would only make it harder for me to leave. Once I was fully dressed, she came to me.

Nicole hadn't put back on her necklace that she used to prevent vampires from controlling her mind. She wanted to show me that she trusted me not to manipulate her. I pulled her to me for one last kiss before leaving.

"Will I see you again?" she asked.

"You'll see me again," I assured. "If that's what you want."

"That is what I want."

"Good. Be careful when you go out. The Ravens are dangerous and they will kill you. Might be a good idea to wear your necklace at all times."

I had told her all about the Ravens. I also told her to keep it to herself. She promised me she would. I believed her. She had no reason to lie to me.

"All right. I will. Call me sometimes," she said.

"Wait, I don't have your number." I took my phone out of my pocket and turned it back on.

All kinds of voicemails and text messages from my mom and dad immediately notified me. I ignored it and as she gave me her phone number, I saved it.

"I got you locked in now." I smiled down at her.

She smiled back. We kissed again and I left out the front door of her apartment.

I walked through the busy streets of the city. The sun was still up and I could enjoy the warmth of the sunrays. The sun wouldn't go down for another two hours, but it still felt good to catch it while it was still up. As I walked around, I observed humans until it was nearly dark.

Humans fascinated me. I wondered what it was like to be like them. I was in no rush to get back home. I didn't care. It was so boring there since I couldn't entertain company. What else was I supposed to do? There was so much more life on the outside. I imagined being human, going about everyday life without having to hide in the shadows of a vampire kingdom. *What did it feel like to grow old? What did it feel like to have such freedom?*

To be free away from Pigalle Palace was something I liked to do. I wanted to be one of the elite to have the blessing of possessing freedom. I wanted to do what I wanted, whenever I wanted, without caring about the consequence. I wanted to be in control of my life. Humans seemed to have that and I envied it.

I was about to cross the street when I saw an elderly woman with her walking stick in one hand and a bag of groceries in the other. She looked worn and weak as she struggled with the bag. She lost her grip on the bag and her groceries fell and spilled out into the street. An apple rolled away and fell into the sewer.

"Shit," she cursed.

People kept walking, stepping over her groceries as if they didn't see that she needed help. What kind of humans were they, too busy to help an elderly woman in need? That was shameful and interesting all at the same time.

I walked over to the old woman. I picked up her things and helped her out of the street.

"Here you go."

She smiled at me and replied, "Thank you. Thank you so much, young man."

"No problem. You close to home?"

"A block up. I'm trying to hurry. It's not safe out here when the night falls. These crazy wolf attacks are happening lately at nightfall. I'm sure a strong man like you could kill a wolf with your bare hands."

It wasn't wolves that were leaving the city in fear. It was the Ravens. They were frightening the whole town. The look in her eyes was fear and sadness wrapped all into one and hit a place in my heart. Suddenly, I cared and I wanted to help the city. I didn't care about the Ravens before I saw the look in that woman's eyes. I realized I had to help my family make this city safe again. It was an emergency.

"I'll walk you home." I put her groceries back into her bag and carried it.

"That's sweet of you. Thank you."

We walked, made small talk about random things like her favorite TV shows and what she was going to make for dinner. It was a beautiful and short conversation. When we were outside her house, I took a few glances to make sure she was safe. It was a cozy brick home with a fenced-in garden. Everything was going to be okay.

"Thank you so much, dear. May God bless you and keep you from harm's way," she said.

I smiled at her. "No problem, you have a good night."

"Can I trouble you again?"

"No problem. What do you need?"

"Can you help me inside? I can't really see when it gets this dark out and looks like I forgot to turn on my lights."

I wondered what she would've done if I hadn't walked her home. I continued being a gentleman. I followed her to her front door. The house was warm and nicely decorated once inside. I turned on her lights and helped her take the groceries out the bag before

I left. She tried to hand me some money when I was done, but I declined.

"Bless you," she said.

"You have a good night."

I walked out of her house and went back to the street. I suddenly felt my hunger rise. What was I going to eat? I didn't want to go back home to eat, but there was no way I was going to hunt and feed on an innocent human. So, what else was I going to do? It wasn't as if I could go to a vampire blood lab. I only heard stories about how Vaisseau had one available. I wished it were still up and running. If I were King, I would definitely want to make Club Vaisseau ours again.

I walked past a dark alleyway. Loud groans and shuffling echoed. The air wasn't right. Someone was in trouble.

Entering the alleyway, I suddenly wished I hadn't. What I saw boiled my blood. It was a female vampire sucking the life out of a little boy. He looked to be no older than ten years old. She must've been a Raven, I thought to myself. I felt my fangs emerge as I approached the redheaded vampire with long flowing hair. She was so busy feasting that she hadn't noticed that I was behind her. I placed my hand on her shoulder. She pulled her fangs out of the human's delicate neck and looked at me with fire in her eyes. My own eyes became fiery. The sight of the blood oozing out of the boy's neck made my hunger intensify. The smell of his blood made my mouth water.

She dropped the boy and pushed me into the wall. I arched my back and moaned. She was strong. I used my strength to force her against the wall. Her nails met my back and dug in. I grabbed her hair roughly, exposing her neck. I jammed my fangs into her skin. I heard her groan in pain, but I ignored it as I snapped her neck. She fell to the ground with a loud thud. I walked over to the human boy to make sure he wasn't dead. It was too late to save him. He was already gone.

I ran my hands down his pale cheeks. As the smell of his blood became more pungent, my hunger really started getting to me. He was already dead and his blood would spill out into the alley anyway. While his blood was still warm, I sank my fangs into his soft tender skin and drank what blood he had left inside of him.

A loud snap startling me echoed through the alleyway. I stood up and turned slowly to see my father and uncle Legend glaring at me as if I had lost my mind. I had sucked the blood of a lifeless young boy. Blood was all over my mouth and two bodies were resting at my feet.

I wiped my mouth and immediately started to explain, "It's not what it looks like. This Raven killed him. It was too late to save his life and I was hungry so…"

"Do I look stupid to you? Rain will rip your heart out when he finds out," my father said. "You had no business leaving the Palace in the first place!"

I wanted to run, but I hadn't gained my strength up enough to run away from them. Not feeding for that many hours was my own fault. I had been caught up with Nicole and then I people-watched for far too long.

We heard another sound down the other side of the alley. We fled and headed home in a flash, undetectable by the human eye before waiting around to see who was there.

I was in a lot of trouble. How was I going to explain this to Uncle Rain if my own father didn't believe me?

CHAPTER 13

ULYSSES

When we got back to the Château, the household was waiting for us in the grand room where Uncle Rain's throne was. He was seated with Aunt Essence next to him. My mother, Aunt Azura, and an unfamiliar face were all glaring at me. I assumed she was the Prototype Legend had brought back from Antigua. Everyone seemed to be in a funk and I knew it was because I had disobeyed the Covenant once again.

"I found him in Paris, sucking the blood of a young boy," my father explained.

Rain put up his hand. "Ulysses can speak for himself, Onyx."

I cleared my throat. My father released his hold on my arm and went to my mother's side.

"Speak, boy!" Rain demanded.

I felt insulted that he called me a boy. I was a grown-ass man.

I straightened up and held my head high. "I only went into Paris to visit a friend of mine. Since you made her leave the other night, I wanted to see her again. After my visit, on my way back home, I came face to face with a Raven in the alley killing this young boy. I fought her, but it was too late to save him. The boy was dead and I was hungry, so I drank his blood."

Suddenly, Rain rose and walked over to me. He took his sword from his side and rammed it into my chest, missing my heart. I coughed out blood the deeper the sword went. I felt like I was dying as my insides began to burn. The sword had been dipped in silver. Though he couldn't kill me because I was a Pureblood, he was making me feel the pain. The silver burned like hell.

He looked at me with disgust and asked, "How could you be so stupid?"

I glared at him, holding my chest. He removed the sword. I continued coughing. I looked down at my own blood as it splattered into my hand.

I gasped for air. "I didn't kill him…"

"You must learn your place, boy. You are destined to be King one day. You don't do stupid things like wandering around aimlessly in the city." He stood over me and I tried to scoot away, but the pain in my chest was killing me. I felt my eyes water, yet I refused to cry. There was no way I was going to show him any more weakness. "You will do exactly as I say from now on. If you don't, I'll be forced to do something to you that I don't want to do… I will behead you if I have to."

My mother gasped before she quickly held her hand over her mouth. My father placed his arms around her. I looked over at my parents and realized my behavior was causing the family some problems that we didn't need to have.

I managed to say, "Okay. I won't do it again."

"If I allow you to bring this woman into the Château to visit, will that keep you here?"

He was trying to compromise with me. He recognized that I had a weakness for a mortal, the way that he had. He saw in me what he saw in himself.

"Yes," I replied.

Though that was my answer, I wasn't absolutely sure that would work. What if I got bored with Nicole? Would he allow other mortal women to come see me? Would I be able to have my parties again?

"Get out of my sight. I don't want to look at you any longer."

I got up quickly as my wound began to heal. It was still causing me a lot of pain, so I clutched it tightly. I headed to my bedroom. As I settled onto my bed, a knock was on the door. Before I could answer, the door opened and my mother entered with two tall gold cups on a golden tray.

"Here, I brought you something," she said with warmth in her tone. "You must be starving."

My mother had been given the right name. Soleil, like the sun, was always so warm and caring. She was an excellent mother—the best anyone could ask for. She set the tray on the side of my bed. I was still hungry. Servants collected blood from donors and kept it in the Château. It wasn't available to all the vampires. That blood was for the Royals. It was up to the vampires to get their own blood slaves. I felt that was another reason why the Ravens were doing whatever they wanted to get blood. They didn't want to be bothered with blood slaves because they acted like mindless zombies.

"Thank you, Mother."

She nodded. "You know I believe what you said earlier about what happened in that alley. You are not a monster. I raised you the right way. Rain knows you didn't kill that boy, too. He wanted to show you that there would be consequences when you disobey him."

I rubbed my sore chest, took a deep breath, and exhaled. "I understand."

"We love you, but don't let your curiosity get the best of you. Soon, the Ravens will be gone and you'll be able to move around a little better. For now, you have to follow the rules."

"All right," I sighed.

"Were you with a woman?" I could tell she really didn't want to ask that question, but she was my mother. Mothers worried about their sons when another woman was involved.

"Yes."

"Are you falling in love with her?"

"It's too soon to tell," I replied. "I enjoy her company. Is there anything wrong with that?"

"Be careful. Mortals have done nothing but bring problems to this family." She placed a motherly kiss on my forehead before leaving me alone.

As I stared up at the ceiling, I thought about Nicole. Though I had left her a few moments ago, I was missing her already. I took my phone out of my pocket and I sent her a text.

I made it home safe. ☺

Within seconds, she texted: *Good. I was thinking about you.* ☺

I smiled to myself.

Another knock on the door halted me from replying to her.

"Come in!"

The Prototype with the lavender eyes walked in. I sat up and stared at her, wondering what she wanted. I thought maybe Legend was with her, but she was alone. She had come to my room alone. She saw the look of confusion on my face and began to speak.

"Ulysses, I came to introduce myself…" She stood at the door. "I'm Mirage Oleander and I'm…"

"A Prototype. The last living Prototype." I eased off the bed and walked over to her. I shook her hand. "It's nice to meet you, Mirage."

"I see that you've done your homework."

"No, not at all. The walls are too thin around here. I hear everything."

"Ah, well, I was intrigued when I heard about you. You're a Pureblood like your great-grandparents. Usually, a Pureblood can only come from two Prototypes… But, you…you were born to two ordinary vampires…"

I interrupted her, "I was born to two half-blooded vampires. I'm rare. I've heard this all my life. To keep it real, none of it means shit to me."

"It should mean everything to you and I'm here to tell you why. When the first two Purebloods were born, Allemand and Christione, we discovered that they were more powerful than Prototypes. As the two of them grew rapidly, we saw the most incredible things. Not only could they move objects with the lift of their fingers, but they were also Daywalkers. That was something we couldn't do and it was like some sort of miracle that they could. We were cursed by the Night and they weren't. For that, we crowned Allemand once he married Christione. This was our first royal family. They gave birth to Valerie, but for some reason, she was born human. How could two Purebloods create a human? It was shocking. She was whisked away, hidden somewhere safe, and she married a vampire to conceive half-breeds of her own. It was predicted that one of her children would be a Daywalker... This made Rain the Divine One. He has done his job of saving vampires from the Préfet, but his job is temporary. So, now that you are a man, you are to be King. You do understand that, right?"

There had to be some mistake. I was told that as long as Rain was living, I was never to be King.

"Rain is King," I replied.

"He is for now, but your bloodline overrules his. Purebloods aren't only very strong and handsome; they are the most eye-catching, breathtaking beings known to man. Purebloods are very dangerous to all vampires, even Prototypes. Your blood can kill us if we drink it. We will die from the inside out. So, you see, as long as there is a Pureblood, he is to be the King."

I stared at her, feeling so confused. I had to take into consideration that she had been one of the first vampires to exist, but I wasn't ready to be King.

"I hear you," I said. "Does Rain know any of this?"

She smiled knowingly. "I'm sure he does."

This was all too overwhelming. I suddenly became nervous. *What did she want me to do? Take over the throne right now?*

"Relax," she said. "Focus on that later. Right now, he needs your help. He won't be able to stop the Ravens without you. Their strength is no match for yours." She smiled before turning to leave me with my thoughts.

I held my head up high. I was about to be King. That meant I would be able to do whatever I pleased. I rubbed my chin. I started thinking of ways to change Pigalle Palace for the better, but first, we were going to have to get rid of the Ravens.

CHAPTER 14

LEGEND

MiMi entered my bedroom unannounced and she did so quietly. I was watching a little TV while sitting on my bed when the door opened. I needed to take my mind off what I saw Rain do to Ulysses. I never wanted to see that happen again. Ulysses was going to get his act together, even if that meant I had to be on his every move. MiMi walked in and up to my bed as if I invited her. I wasn't expecting to see her because Rain made it clear that she was to stay in her own room.

"What's up?" I asked while getting up. "Is everything okay?"

She stood right in front of me. One of her hands touched the very ends of one of my dreads. Then, without warning, she pushed me on my bed. My back hit the mattress and I stared up at her to see a smile coming to her face.

"What are you doing?" I asked.

Her hand caressed my chest, up and down before unbuttoning my shirt. She straddled my waist and slowly leaned down. She started kissing my lips seductively. She was too sexy to resist. I wrapped my left hand around her waist, and with my right hand, I placed my hand in her hair. I stroked and massaged her scalp. She stared intensely into my eyes.

She kissed my neck and licked it. I felt the tingly sensation, but I couldn't let her have me. We had to be married first and as much as I wanted to break the rules, we had to stop. I removed my hands from her.

"What's the matter? You don't want me?" she questioned.

"I do want you, but not like this... If what you tell me is true about being my wife, then we have to wait until our wedding night to make love."

She eased off me and nodded her head slowly, almost sadly. "When will you be ready to be married?"

I shrugged. I really didn't know because I was still getting to know her. I wanted to take my time. I wasn't going to make her wait forever, but I needed a little more time.

"Soon," I said. "I mean that...very soon."

"Come for a walk with me," she stated.

"Where are we going?"

"Come on!"

She got up from the bed and reached for my hand. I got up and took her hand. MiMi smiled at me lovingly. I smiled back at her. Her beauty was intoxicating and it was tough not to give into temptation, but I remained firm.

We walked out of the bedroom and down the hall, hand in hand.

"I want to show you something," she said.

"All right."

She led me down the long corridor and down a set of stairs. We walked to the farthest part of the east wing in silence. The whole time, I kept wondering where we were going. On the other side of the kitchen, there was a slender door. I hadn't noticed that door before, but there were so many doors in the palace, it would be easy to overlook this one. She opened it and it was dark inside, but I could see a spiral staircase going down. She walked down before me and I followed her reluctantly. It was so dark, but our eyes could see everything.

When we reached the bottom of the staircase, there was a set of massive stone double doors at the end of the room. Was this were the tombs were? I looked at her. She ran her hand over the side of the door that looked like a lock. It resembled the pieces I had seen around Rain's and Essence's necks.

"So this is where they are," I said.

She nodded. "Yes...King Allemand, Queen Christione, and Princess Valerie lie behind these doors." Tiny tears came to her eyes.

"How come you haven't told Rain?"

"Because he already knows and he's afraid. He found them a while ago."

"Why would he be afraid?" I scowled.

She looked at me. "Once he and Queen Essence open this door, King Allemand and Queen Christione will rise. They are only sleeping. Purebloods can never be killed, only bound by this tomb and only awakened by their predecessor."

I swallowed hard. "What about our mother? Will she rise too?"

Mirage shook her head sadly. "No. She was human, so her body has already turned to ashes. Rain doesn't want to wake them without her. His memories of her are precious memories that he will forever hold on to. He's very selfish right now. Power has gone to his head. It's important for you all to know everything and that's why I'm here. There will be no more secrets."

"If Rain opens the door, what will happen once they're awakened?"

"Once they are awakened, Ulysses will be crowned King and he will have his ancestors at his side."

I processed what she was saying. The Purebloods would be united and Rain would no longer be King. I wondered if Rain's own selfishness wouldn't allow him to open up this door for that reason. He was enjoying having that power position.

"What if Rain never opens it?"

"That's the part I'm not sure about, but the Divination was misinterpreted by the Préfet purposely. King Allemand wrote it in a way that confused them. Yes, it spoke of a Divine One and of an heir to the throne, but it also said that when it was time, King Allemand, himself, would crown the King. Rain was crowned by the Préfet, which made his days of ruling temporary. He was given the keys to guard and was given instructions. Together, he and Queen Essence will open this door. Since Ulysses is fully grown, he can now be King and the Divination will be complete."

I let her words soak in. I wasn't so sure that Ulysses was ready. He was still so immature.

Reading my mind, MiMi said, "With the guide of your grandfather, he will be fine."

I hoped Rain would do what was right. I would be too afraid to go against the Divination. I thought about how the keys mysteriously disappeared from around their necks before MiMi and I came back from Antigua. Rain had no intentions of opening up this tomb. I suddenly became worried.

MiMi held my hand in hers as she said, "Don't worry. Soon, Ulysses will know the truth and Rain will have to obey."

Suddenly, a feeling came over me. The longer I looked into her eyes, the more aroused I grew. She was turning me on standing there. I didn't know if it was because she was so real with me, or what, but I aggressively took her into my arms and gave her a lust-filled kiss. I moaned as she pushed her tongue inside of mine. I grabbed a fistful of her hair and groaned as I tugged on it. I practically ripped off her clothes as I pressed her up against the wall. She helped me to remove my shirt and then my pants. I stood in front of her in my boxers.

She admired the muscles in my stomach and eyed my body hungrily. She then grabbed my dreads and pulled them as I pushed her up against the wall. I tilted her head back as she arched her neck toward me. I licked my bottom lip as I felt my fangs elongate. I leaned down to kiss her neck gently, trailing her soft flesh. I felt the need to bite her. I wanted to taste her.

"Once you drink from me, we are bonded...soul mates," she said, reading my thoughts.

I let my fangs penetrate her skin. I moaned as her blood slid down my throat. I felt the instant feeling of love. What I was fighting, I could no longer fight. She was mine and I was hers. I enjoyed the sensation of her. Her blood was sweet.

She moved her hands down to my boxers and placed her hands inside to feel how hard I was. She rubbed it roughly; ready to have me inside of her.

I pulled my fangs away and licked my bloodied lips, savoring the taste of her. She looked at my lips before kissing me passionately. Her tongue brushed up against mine and I sucked it. My soul was telling me this was right and she was everything she said she was. She moaned and closed her eyes and when she looked at me again, there was so much pleasure in them.

"I want you," I said as I watched her breathe deeply.

I could feel how badly I wanted her. I let her stroke me. I wanted her to do whatever she wanted and however she wanted it. She lifted her leg to go around my waist. I lifted the other and held her up by her thighs. I was centered correctly. I placed myself inside of her with her back still resting against the wall. I thrust into her deeply.

She moaned.

I moved in and out of her as she breathed against the side of my face. With both of her hands clasping the back of my head, I moved deeper and faster until I was fucking her hard against that wall. As our bodies glided in a perfect rhythm with one another, I made her cum over and over and over again. Her moans bounced off the walls. I didn't stop until we both had the final orgasm.

CHAPTER 15

AZURA

I dived into one of the two swimming pools that were in the Château, wearing a black bikini. I stretched my arms and legs while I swam indoors peacefully. I liked the feeling of the water as it caressed me. It made me think of the way Claude's hands felt as he fondled me. I shook him out of my head. I was forbidden from ever seeing him again. I enjoyed my swim, freeing my mind of all the bad shit that was starting to happen. It was this pure pleasure that brought a slight smile to my face.

No matter how hard I tried to swim my thoughts away, I couldn't get my mind off Claude. I really needed to say goodbye and at least tell him that what he had done the other night was a mistake. I needed closure. I couldn't blame Rain for being angry with me for what I had done with Claude or for punishing Ulysses in front of all of us. It was something we all needed to be brought back to the reality that this was our new life. What we were doing was playing a dangerous game that could threaten what Rain was trying to build as the King.

When I was done swimming, I got out and took a towel to dry off. I went to my room and picked out a black dress that wrapped around my body with the back out. The dress was very skimpy, but that was the point. If I was going to be saying goodbye to Claude, then I was going to have to make it a good one. I let my hair dry in its natural waves on its own. I painted my lips with red lipstick. I put on some mascara and a little eye shadow. I finished my look with some red heels and a red clutch.

I was going to have to sneak out, especially with Rain banning me from Vaisseau. As much as I wanted to tell him what I was going to do, he wouldn't stand for it. I was going to end this with Claude. He didn't have anything to worry about me. I drove one of the cars to the club because I didn't want one of the drivers to know where I was going.

I went to the Red Light District with a scattered brain. I was trying to play out what I was going to say to Claude and how I was going to leave if he attempted to kiss me. I parked the car in the busy parking lot. I walked down the alley quickly. As soon as I was at Vaisseau's doors, the doorman recognized me and let me in without speaking. When I walked into the club, the music was pumping and everybody was dancing.

This rush of good energy hit me and it hit me hard. I was going to miss coming down here.

I didn't see Claude right away, so I went over to the bar, aware of all the eyes on me as I ordered a drink. I thought I might as well enjoy a drink while waiting for him. The bartender gave me a wink and I slightly smiled at him. I looked around everywhere. I could see the usual vampires trying to satisfy their needs with mortals.

I took my gaze off them and continued to search for Claude.

After a while of searching with my eyes, I finished my drink. My eyes zoomed in on Claude near the VIP area. Seeing him again sent a chill down my spine.

Why did he have to be the most gorgeous and delicious-looking man I had ever seen?

I stood up and made my way to the dance floor to get to him. The vampires surrounding him backed away as if I was the goddess that Claude had been waiting for.

The moment his eyes landed on mine, I couldn't help but bite my bottom lip. My soul purred. I didn't want it to. Never has my soul purred like this before. *Ever.*

He came to me the way a man did when he saw his lover enter the room. He invaded my personal space as he always did. When he gripped my hips tightly and buried his head into the crook of my neck to inhale my scent, I tried to back away, but his dominance was high. I had never felt that way with any other vampire and Claude had a way of bringing me into his world once again. I snapped out of my thoughts when I felt his lips brush up against my neck.

"Can we go somewhere less crowded to talk, please?" I whispered.

His lips curved into a snide smirk. "Sure." He nodded and let go of me.

I grabbed his hand and turned from the VIP before I took him upstairs. We went into a room that was unoccupied and closed the door.

"How can I help you?" he asked.

"I came here to tell you that I can no longer see you anymore. This will be your last time seeing me in Vaisseau unless you stop the Ravens from the unnecessary killings."

"Is this some sort of an ultimatum?" he asked with his eyes widening.

"Not really… But, I would like to be able to see you again. The only way I can do that is if you stop being so evil."

"I don't do ultimatums."

I was hoping that he would say that he was falling in love with me and that he would do whatever it took to keep seeing me. That didn't happen. Claude was firm in what he believed.

"Well, then, you leave me no other choice. I can't be seen around here or with you anymore. Rain is making plans as we speak to shut all of this down. I wouldn't want to be in the middle of that. My loyalty is to my brother first and foremost."

Claude erupted into laughter. "That's seriously too bad."

Feeling myself growing angrier with each second of him laughing, I turned to walk out of the room quickly, but he stood in front of the door. Suddenly, two other vampires came into the room from another door near the back of the room. They were surrounding me. I had no other way out.

"Looks like you're not going anywhere," he said.

His men grabbed me.

"Let me go!" I screamed, grabbing their hands, trying to scratch them.

They had me—one man on one arm and one man on the other. They were too strong to fight off. I yelled again. I didn't have time to curse obscenities. Claude snapped my neck and the ground rose up to catch me at an alarming speed. Darkness welcomed me.

CHAPTER 16

AZURA

felt pain. My limbs were numb and aching. I could barely move a muscle without feeling sore. I fluttered my eyelashes open to find that I was bound to a wooden chair in the center of the room. My feet were chained to the floor and my hands were tied tightly behind my back. I started trembling in fear.

Claude spoke, "Well, Ravens, what shall I do with Princess Azura?" He smiled coldly.

I looked up to see that ten other vampires, all Ravens, surrounded me. They were peering at me cautiously. I had no idea what was going on, but I needed to get out of there. What was he going to do with me? They were all whispering, looking at one another.

"I think I should kill her… I mean…it would be a perfect way to get Rain to show his face. Then, I can tell him that the Ravens aren't going anywhere. We are only going to grow more powerful and stronger than anything he has ever seen. We will be too strong for him to stop. Soon, all of Paris will be ours. No more humans."

"How will you feed if there are no more humans in Paris?"

"There are tons of cities throughout France, Azura. You seem like a smart girl. We will grow and grow." Claude laughed with pure evil. "In the meantime, I have to figure out how I'm going to kill you. I really don't want to. I really wanted you to be my lover and join us, but that would've never worked."

I struggled with my hands to try to get them free, but it was no use. I wasn't going anywhere. "Let me go, Claude. I won't come back down here ever again and you can go on and do what it is that you do."

"You shouldn't have come back here tonight. I would've gotten the hint that you had fun while it lasted. Nevertheless, you came here and threatened me as if I was supposed to tell the Ravens to back down. We don't back down for nobody." Claude took a switchblade from his pocket and traced my face with it. "You're so beautiful... It's a shame that I have to cut your head off."

I tried my best to move my face away, but I couldn't because the chair was restricting me.

"Please, let me go!"

"Chain her to the wall," Claude ordered.

Two men took hold of my arms and untied me from the chair. They took me over to the wall where chains were. They chained both arms up above my head and chained my feet to the wall. I swallowed hard. Suddenly, Claude slit both of my wrists. Blood oozed out. I panicked when I wasn't healing. He must've given me a serum to stop me from healing. What was he trying to do? Make me bleed to death? Or was he torturing me?

I cried. He smiled at me while lifting my head to look into his eyes.

"Azura, soon, all of your precious little blood is going to leave your body and your brother will have no choice but to finally face me. Are you ready to die?"

CHAPTER 17

RAIN

I heard a soft knock on my bedroom door.

"Come in," I said.

"Your highness, your car awaits you," my personal butler said.

I heard him. I sat up in bed. It was time for me to make my appearance at Vaisseau. It was a dreaded visit, but it was long overdue and the only way to find out what was really going on was to go down there.

"I'll be down in a moment. Wait for me downstairs."

He left. I walked toward the window. I lifted the Victorian curtain enough to see that the moon was shining bright. I let out a deep sigh. Essence got out of bed.

"I'm coming with you," she asserted.

I stared at her shortly. She had what it took to do well. If I told her no, she would chase after me anyway. Essence had a bit of my power from when I had transformed her. She would be able to hold her own if she came along.

"All right. The car is waiting."

She was my life and my love and when nothing else mattered, she did. I wanted nothing more than to have her at my side.

I opened the door and went downstairs. She was right with me.

"Are you going down there now?" Legend questioned as soon as we reached the bottom of the stairs.

I stared at him as Mirage stuck firmly by his side. The violet lace dress that she was wearing made her violet eyes even more vibrant. One thing was for certain; she refused to leave his side. We never saw Legend alone since she got here. Legend hadn't said anything about when they were going to get married, but looking at them, they had already bonded. It was his life and I had other things to worry about.

"Yes, Essence and I are going to check things out."

"Do you need me to come?" Legend asked.

"No. We won't be long."

"Wait," Ulysses said as he jogged down the stairs. "If you're going to the Club, I need to go with you."

Rain looked at Ulysses up and down. "This is not a trip to go and play, Ulysses. I'm going to handle business."

"We have to do this together. The Ravens are deep in number and there is no way you can take them alone. I have to come."

"He's right," Mirage spoke up. "Ulysses has to go."

This day would come. The day, when Ulysses would be ready for his crown, was upon me. I could've yelled, screamed, and told him to stay back, but the Ravens would be too much for me to handle on my own. I clenched my teeth together and replied, "Let's go."

As much as I dreaded this day, I was going to have to face it.

We proceeded quickly to the limo. We were in the back and the door was closed. As the car pulled around the circular driveway, I stared out of the tinted window at the night. I chose to be silent and they didn't try to break it up. My thoughts were too heavy. Not only was I thinking about a way to stop this madness with the Ravens, but also I was thinking about what life would be like with Ulysses on the throne.

I felt he wasn't ready, but tonight, he was going to have to prove it to me.

We arrived momentarily and got out of the car. The driver parked the car on the other side of the alley and waited for us. We stood in line and waited to be let inside. Once inside, the energy immediately felt different. The music was blasting so loud that it made my sensitive ears ache a little. It had been a long time since I'd been in a club, but the music seemed to be extra loud. It was crowded and full of those pathetic creatures, dancing and jumping around. *Ravens.*

I still couldn't believe that there were so many of them, but when vampires lose themselves, they are so lost that they become heartless and rebel. Nothing is on their minds except to kill. Essence nearly became one during her Newborn stage. I was glad she came to her senses. I noticed the way she had her nose turned up at them.

Ulysses stared around the room bravely. Purebloods were born with many gifts. He could destroy everyone in here with the lift of his finger. He could rip their hearts from their chests in a blink of an eye. The disgusted look on his face let me know that he didn't approve either.

I looked back around the club. Everyone was doing different things. A woman was dancing wildly on the bar. A live band was on the stage, giving a rock performance. Those that weren't getting a drink at the bar were dancing to the band.

I noticed a vampire sitting coolly in the VIP area. He had dark hair, blue eyes, and a muscular body.

"Stay right here," I told Essence and Ulysses.

They did what I told them as I walked over to the VIP. His eyes landed on me and a smirk appeared on his face. He signaled for his men to let me in. I observed the two men carefully and walked on the other side of the ropes.

"Ah, King Rain, what brings you here?" he asked.

"You know why I'm here."

His eyes darkened, turning to a dark blue as he stood up from the couch. "You came to tell me that every vampire would be free to do as they please?"

I put my hand around his neck and squeezed until he began to lift off his feet. "Of course not. I'm here to let you know that your days of ruling the Ravens are over."

Claude had a look of surprise on his face at how strong I was. I kept squeezing. One of his men stabbed me in my back. I lost my grip around his neck and he fled. The men fled with him and disappeared somewhere in the club. I removed the dagger and threw it on the ground. Essence and Ulysses rushed to me.

"They went upstairs," Ulysses said.

We eased through the crowd that kept right on dancing with the band. We went upstairs, and then went right and then left. Things had changed so much that I wasn't sure I would be able to find my way along the corridors as the wound in my back healed.

Something stopped me in my tracks. I felt something was wrong in my gut. I could smell my sister's scent and it was strong. It was the scent of her blood. Azura was dying.

Ulysses said, "Azura's in trouble."

"She's in one of these rooms," I said.

CHAPTER 18

LEGEND

"This isn't right!" Onyx shouted as he slammed his hands on the round table. "You and I should be down there with them!"

Onyx's chest heaved in and out. Soleil tried to comfort him by putting her hand on his shoulder, but he pulled away. He wanted to protect Ulysses more than anything and he would be upset if something happened to him.

MiMi spoke delicately. "Onyx, your son is a Pureblood. He will make sure that they all will return in one piece. I assure you that."

I frowned once I realized I hadn't seen our sister since earlier. "Where's Azura?" I asked. "Is she in her room?" I went up the stairs and down the hall to find her bedroom was empty. She wasn't there. I returned to the table. "She's gone."

"I hope she didn't go down to Vaisseau," Soleil said. "Does Rain know she's there?"

"If he didn't know when he left, he's about to find out," Onyx said. "So what do we do? Wait here until they return?"

"That's all we can do. Rain wanted us to stay here," I answered.

MiMi walked over to the window and stared out at the dark sky. Thunder lit up the sky.

"A huge storm is coming," she said.

Whenever a storm came, it always connected to Rain's strong emotions. This was going to be it. Rain was going to end the Ravens' reign.

CHAPTER 19

ESSENCE

After opening nearly every door on the top floor of Vaisseau, every room was empty as if Claude had warned them that we were there. We came to the door that used to be the office. I could smell the scent of Azura's blood intensified as we stood outside it.

"She's in here," I said. "I can smell her."

Rain tried the door, but it was locked. He kicked it down and barged inside. No one was inside, but Azura's limp body was chained to the wall. Her head was hanging to the side. A massive amount of her blood was like a pool under her feet.

I gasped at the sight of her. Rain was at Azura's side in a flash. As he lifted her chin, we could clearly see that all her life had been drained from her. Tears emerged from Rain's eyes and he shouted, "Fuck! We're too late."

Ulysses balled up his fists angrily and I couldn't hold in my own cries. Claude had killed her. Rain broke her chains to release her. Azura rested in his arms.

He caressed her hair as he cried, "My dear sister… My dear sister… Essence, you must get her home. I want you to take her home!"

I wept as I responded, "All right."

I took Azura from him and tossed her over my shoulder. Instead of going out the front door, I jumped out of the window and landed on my feet. I didn't want to have to fight on my way out. I ran around to the front of the club where the limo was waiting. I slid Azura's body inside.

"Take us home," I said to the driver.

I held Azura close to me as we rode back. It seemed like such a long ride. I could only imagine the rage Rain was feeling. I, too, wanted to kill Claude. I wept for Azura. As I stared down at her motionless face, I could only imagine what kind of torture it was to feel her blood leave her body.

Once we arrived home, I carried her out of the car and into the house.

"Legend! Onyx!" I shouted as I laid Azura down in the middle of the floor.

Everyone came rushing into the room.

"What happened to her?" Soleil asked as she gasped.

Fresh tears emerged from my eyes. "She's dead… Claude… He killed her… She bled to death."

Legend knelt down by his sister with a look of anguish. Soleil wrapped herself in Onyx's arms as they cried together.

"Where are Ulysses and Rain?" Legend asked.

"They're still there. Claude disappeared, so they're going to find him."

"I need to go down there!" Onyx asserted angrily.

"If you go, I'm coming with you," Legend said, rising to his feet.

None of us was going to stop them. We wanted revenge for Azura's death. They left the Château, leaving Mirage, Soleil, and me alone with Azura's body.

"I can't believe this…" I sniffled.

"When my brother, Evan, was murdered, I felt this pain that I can't describe." Mirage knelt down beside me and said, "Being a vampire was something you never wanted… But, it brought you a family you always needed."

I hadn't thought of that. I struggled with accepting this life, mainly because I missed being human. When I was human, I had no family. My mom and dad gave me up for adoption and I didn't know the first place to look to find them. The only motherly figure I had was Joanne. Mirage was right. I now had a husband, brothers, sisters, and a nephew. They embraced me and loved me. I was their family and they were mine. That was something that I needed to hear.

I nodded as I picked up Azura's limp hand. "Thank you, Mirage."

It was time for me to move past my pain at no longer being mortal. Soleil took Azura's other hand in hers as she wept silently.

"You're welcome." Mirage rubbed my shoulder and said, "Azura will always be with us."

I kissed Azura's forehead and we waited for the family to return.

CHAPTER 20

ULYSSES

When we came down the stairs, we noticed the club was nearly empty. We stood in the middle of the dance floor. There was no bartender and no band playing. A few more people were leaving as if someone told them to get out and to get out fast. We heard a loud click of the front door once the last person was out. Without the bodies in the club, the atmosphere turned cold. I looked over at Rain. He was waiting to see how many of them would appear. The Ravens were still inside. We could hear them moving around.

We heard a single pair of loud footsteps echoing as he walked through the door to the main floor of the club. As he walked toward us, his eyes didn't shift nor did he blink. He stood a few feet away from us, very still like a pale statue.

"Claude," Rain said, breaking the deafening silence.

"Rain," he muttered through his clenched jaw.

"Why'd you kill my sister?"

"Because I needed your attention, Rain!" he yelled.

I balled up my fist as soon as those words escaped his mouth. Rain put his hand in front of my chest to stop me from pouncing on him. Ten other Ravens came from out the shadows. Some were standing above us while the others surrounded us. They didn't come too close, but it was close enough to let us know that we were outnumbered.

"Now that I'm here, now what?" Rain asked calmly.

"I'll let the both of you leave untouched if you leave right now. What we are doing is unavoidable and unstoppable," he replied in a gentler tone. "That's something you're going to have to deal with."

"As your King, you are ordered to stop."

"As my *King?*" Claude chuckled. "That's funny. The Ravens have no King. We follow no rules, ain't that right?"

His brood verbally agreed. I had instant thoughts of how I was going to kill each one of them. I didn't know what Uncle Rain was thinking about doing, but I wasn't going to walk out of there peacefully. They were going to die.

The way Claude's devilish grin was carved into his face and how his black hair was plastered in front of his face as his eyes peeked through it made me want to rip his head off.

"I have to say, I expected you to come down because of what I've done to your sister. You know I didn't have to kidnap her. She came to me and I fucked her so hard before I ended her life. She couldn't stay away from me."

I hated the gloat in his voice. Uncle Rain apparently did, too, because he charged at Claude. They exchanged blows, punching one another viciously. I almost thought of stepping in, but Rain was handling him. Claude tried to step sideways as if he had predicted Rain's next blow, but he stumbled. Rain grabbed him by his neck and threw him across the room. Claude's body slammed into the wall causing the brick to crumble.

Claude looked up with raging eyes. He stood up on his feet quickly. He signaled to the Ravens to step in for him. Some jumped down from the stairs and started charging us with their fists. A surge of anger came from the tip of my toes up to the top of my head in a flash. Thunder sounded and shook the whole club. It felt like an earthquake. That didn't stop me. The Ravens looked around with confusion. Rain looked around at how the chandeliers were shaking and pieces of the ceiling fell.

I put up my hands toward a group of them and a full force of what looked like the wind left my body. I froze them in their tracks.

I had no idea I could freeze anybody. The Ravens stared in shock. I didn't act as if I was surprised by what happened. I did it again and froze the rest of them.

Claude immediately tried to run.

"Where do you think you're going?"

With his back turned away from me, I froze his ass too.

We listened and the building stopped shaking. All was quiet. We could hear no other sounds. I looked over at my uncle.

"Did you know I could do that?" I asked.

He shook his head. "No, I had no idea. Pretty impressive there, nephew." He walked around one of the Ravens and observed them. He used one of his fingers to tap on it. "They're still alive under that ice. Once they thaw, it will be like nothing changed."

I had an idea. "I can fix that." I went to the first frozen statue of one of the Ravens and I punched through the hard ice and reached into his chest. I ripped out his heart, tossing it onto the floor. "He's dead now."

I proceeded to do that to the others while Rain kicked off some of their frozen heads.

Before we could get to Claude, we heard banging on the door. Together, we walked over to check things out. Opening the door cautiously, Legend and my dad walked in with daggers in their hands.

"Y'all all right?" Legend asked.

"Yeah, everyone is dead. We still have Claude left."

They walked in to see the massacre of frozen bodies and dismembered heads.

"Goddamn. Their body parts are frozen?" Onyx said. "How'd that happen?"

"Ulysses, here, has the gift of freezing apparently," Rain said.

"Damn. Well, all right," my dad stated.

"Go ahead and finish off Claude, Ulysses. We aren't leaving him alive."

I walked up to Claude's hard statue and I was more than glad to be the one to take him out. This was for my aunt. I punched through his frozen body and ripped out his heart. I threw it on the ground.

"Anybody left?" Legend asked while looking around.

"I think this is it," I said. "If they are any, they'll be too afraid to do anything now. Their leader is dead."

"What we going to do with the club?" Father asked.

"We're taking it back over," Rain declared. "To make sure nothing like this ever happens again."

I smiled. To know there would be a place where we could get out of the Palace to have a good time made me instantly happy. "I like that."

"Sounds like someone is way too excited about that," my dad stated. "But, I'm down. Soleil misses bartending."

Legend added, "I'm in."

Rain nodded. "Good. Come on, we must get home. We'll come back to clean up this mess later."

I left out of Vaisseau with my uncles and father. The rain was coming down so hard that it soaked our clothes as we ran to get into the limo.

We entered the Château and after walking down the corridor, we found Azura lying in the middle of the floor with Mirage, Essence, and Soleil sitting around her.

"I'll be right back," Uncle Rain said as he went up the stairs.

My mother came to me and hugged me. She was glad to see that I had made it in one piece. Then she went to hug my father. Legend held Mirage's hand.

"What happened? You guys are soaking wet," Essence asked.

"It's a thunderstorm outside," I said. "The rain is coming down really hard. Did you feel the earthquake?"

"What earthquake?" Legend asked.

They all looked confused. It dawned on me that my anger caused the building to shake like that. No one else felt it but the ones that were inside the club. My strength was greater than I thought.

Onyx said, "When Rain gets angry, he can make a storm happen. I guess with the two of you together, it created a thunderstorm."

"Oh," I replied.

That was damn cool to me.

Rain returned with medallions that were on these necklaces. I recognized them. They usually were around his neck.

"Legend, pick up Azura. Follow me."

Legend lifted Azura from the floor. We followed him through the Château. This place was huge and I hadn't seen half of it. He led us to the farthest part of the east wing of this door. No one spoke or said a word. We all traveled down the spiral staircase and approached a set of double doors made out of stone.

"Is this...?" My father nearly gasped with wide eyes.

"This is it," Uncle Rain replied. "This is the tomb where our mother and our grandparents lie... This will be Azura's resting place, too." Rain handed the other key to Essence. "We have to open it together. But, before I do, I have to tell you all something. Once I open this door, King Allemand and Queen Christione will wake up. Purebloods can never ever die. Our mother won't wake up, of course."

We all had heard about the tomb of our ancestors, but I thought it was a story. I didn't think it was real.

Legend nodded, but my father and mother were looking as confused as I was.

"You mean they're not dead?" my father asked.

"No, they're sleeping. Is everyone ready?"

I was nervous. How did he know that this would happen this way? What if it was a trap? Ignoring my fears, I watched carefully as he and Essence put the keys into the lock and unlocked it.

A rumbling sound occurred as the stone doors slid open. Once the doors finished opening completely, a gust of dust eased out causing us all to cough. They opened to reveal a room that was still lit by torches. We walked into the square room and it was spacious enough to fit all of us. Three stone-like coffins sat in the middle of the floor. Their names were etched into the stone: *King Allemand, Queen Christione,* and *Princess Valerie.*

Legend placed Azura next to their tombs. Rain went to Allemand's tomb and slid the top off, placing it on the other side of the room. We all stared inside at his corpse-like body. His wrinkled hands were folded across his chest and he looked as if his body were deteriorating. He was wearing French-inspired royal clothing, nothing less than what I expected to be worn by a King of his stature.

Suddenly, his eyes opened and it scared us all, but he wasn't moving. He was staring directly at me. Out of everyone standing there, why was he staring at me?

"Purebloods must have pure blood. You have to give him your blood, Ulysses," Mirage said when she noticed no one knew what to do. "That will give him the strength that he needs. He only needs a little."

I swallowed the hard lump in my throat. Rain stepped to the side reluctantly. I took a deep breath before walking over to the tomb.

King Allemand's eyes continued to follow me until I was standing right above him.

"Does anyone have a knife?" I asked.

"Here," my father said as he took a dagger out of his back jeans pocket.

I took the dagger nervously in my hand and sliced the inside of my other hand. Mirage took my hand and put it up to my great-grandfather's mouth. He drank from my hand. It only took him a few gulps before he was able to sit up in his coffin. As if magic was performed, he transformed in front of our eyes. He looked so young, trapped at the age of his early twenties. As our elder, he didn't look any older. He stared at each of us with a look of pride.

"Ma famille. Vous êtes tous belle," he uttered in French.

We all could understand him. We didn't speak in French often to one another, but we were still very familiar with the language. He said that we were his family and we were all beautiful.

He took a good look at me and continued, *"Le Roi. Mon arrière petit-fils."*

He recognized me as the King, his great-grandson.

I nodded at him with a grin. Rain opened up Christione's tomb. I gave her my blood to drink. Instantly, Christione rose out of her coffin, looking much like Azura. It was kind of eerie, yet incredible at the same time. Azura was her doppelganger. I passed the painting of her in the hallway and never paid attention to how much they looked alike.

Christione gasped without words as she stared at us in awe. As they regained their strength, Allemand got out of his coffin and helped Christione out of hers.

"Celle Divine," Allemand said as he stared at Rain. Rain bowed before him. Allemand placed his hand on his shoulder. *"Merci."*

"It was an honor and a pleasure, grandfather."

King Allemand's eyes fell upon Azura's body lying on the ground. He clicked his tongue against his teeth. Queen Christione went to her body and stared sadly.

"She was murdered this evening by a Raven. The Ravens have been taken care of," Rain said. "They won't be a problem anymore."

"Put her body in my wife's coffin," Allemand expressed in English with a thick French accent.

Legend picked her body up and placed her in Christione's coffin.

We all stood in a line, waiting to see what would happen next. When Allemand's eyes stopped upon Mirage, they narrowed instantly. He seemed leery as he approached her.

"Mirage Oleander…" Allemand said. "Where is Evan?"

She bowed before him. "He was murdered, your highness. He was only doing what the Préfet instructed. They said that if he didn't put you and Christione in this tomb, they would kill him."

He hummed as he rubbed his chin. "Yet, they killed him anyway."

Mirage lowered her eyes with shame. "Yes, your highness."

"Do you have ill intentions with this family?" He stared deep into her.

She lifted her head high. "No, your highness."

"Good." He walked over to Legend. "You have grown into such a man, Legend. You have taken Mirage to be your wife?"

"Yes, your highness."

Allemand hugged him and then Christione did the same.

"Onyx… You and your wife have given birth to the next King… a Pureblood."

"Yes," my father said. "His name is Ulysses."

Allemand smiled and gave him and my mother a hug. Christione hugged them next.

When Allemand stopped in front of me, he looked deeply into my eyes. I bowed before him. He removed the crown from his own head and placed it on mine. I looked up at him with wide eyes. I had no idea he was going to crown me at that moment.

"A King with your power should never look so afraid. You are the King now and we will do what you say, King Ulysses."

He and Christione bowed before me. Everyone else followed suit. This felt so weird and I was going to have to get used to it. I accepted my fate. As I stared at everyone, I realized that this was what I was born to do. They were going to rely on me to keep this Kingdom running.

"Hail! King Ulysses!" Allemand declared.

"Hail! King Ulysses!" everyone chimed in.

After a few more minutes, we covered Azura's coffin. Uncle Rain stared at Valerie's coffin as if she were going to rise from her grave. Allemand stood beside him.

"She was so beautiful. We will never know why she was born human, but we loved her nonetheless. You will always have your mother in your heart as I will always have my daughter in my heart."

We all walked out of the room. Rain and Essence locked it up.

Rain tried to hand the keys to him.

"No. The key will always belong to you and your wife," Allemand said. "My daughter wanted you to have it. Your mother made me promise that you would be able to keep it because it is connected to your memory of her."

Rain and Essence put their necklaces back around their necks. As we headed back up the stairs, we all were having our own conversations with one another. King Allemand seemed most concerned with talking to me.

"I want you to think about what you're going to do while King. What rules do you want to change? Don't answer that, but think about it. We shall throw a grand event in a few days. Then, we shall discuss with the family how Pigalle Palace is to be."

"All right," I replied, swallowing the hard lump that was in my throat.

I looked over and noticed that Rain was staring, listening to our conversation. I saw the jealousy in his eyes, but it went away as quickly as it came. It was tough for him to step down and allow me to rule before he thought I was ready. I was sure I was going to make mistakes as the new King, but with time, I would be perfect. Then, Rain smiled at me. I smiled back.

CHAPTER 21

ULYSSES

B eing the King of Pigalle Palace wasn't as bad as I thought it would be. We had partied and all the vampires in the Red Light District were invited. We had a blast. Allemand loved to have fun. He was so laid-back and cool. That's what I liked most about him. I spent part of the night talking to Nicole on the phone. I would've loved for her to come, but no mortals were allowed.

The first thing that I changed was I wasn't going to wear that heavy crown. I didn't like the way it felt on my head. I put that in a display case. It was time to get with the new times. Allemand's crown was a family heirloom, so a grand display case was the perfect home for it.

A few weeks later, I sat down with the entire family to discuss what I had already changed.

"Club Vaisseau is opening back up as the family business tonight, but I renamed it to shake off the bad vibes the Ravens have given it. It's now called Club Azura. I took a crew down there and we cleaned it up and did some new decorating."

"I love that name," Essence stated.

"Azura would love it too," Rain added.

The rest of them agreed as I handed them the flyers I already had circulated around the Red Light District.

I continued, "We will all do our part to keep the family business running smoothly. The blood lab will be back running too. I also want to put a blood lab in Paris soon."

They gasped. A murmur of how insane that was filled the room. I put up my hand and they stopped.

"If you don't mind me asking," Allemand said, "why do you want to do that? Vampires are to only remain in the Red Light District."

"Well, for those like myself, with human friends in Paris. I plan to visit them from time to time and I would like access to blood without having to drink from anyone. This will lower the urge to want to kill. Vampires will run it. The lab will have a 'V' symbol to let everyone know that this blood is for vampires only. We will not fool them into thinking it's for anything else."

"So, what you're saying is that you want vampires to be able to roam amongst humans without fear?" Allemand asked.

"Exactly. We make them aware that we are here, but we aren't going to harm them. We are to remain anonymous. When you enter the lab, you go to the front desk and check in. No one will know if you're there to donate or if you're there to get a drink. UV coating will protect the lab so no one will know that vampires are running it with an underground train system that will lead back into the District. When you are let into the back, the donors will be led to a room to give blood and the vampires will be taken to a chamber to be replenished."

"Nothing like this has ever been done," Christione said. "But, I love the idea of that. I'm not comfortable with knowing we will be able to coexist with humans and I'm not sure how they will respond to that either."

"They are already curious. Enough of them come to the Red Light District because they heard about us. Instead of making them forget everyone on their way out of the club, we can make them comfortable around us. They can still decide to give freely like they were doing at the club," I replied.

"Well, we support you," Rain said. "We will give it a try and see how it works."

I smiled.

"Does this mean that we can go into Paris anytime we want?" My mother raised her eyebrows.

"Yes, but if any vampire kills a human being, they will receive the maximum punishment... They will be arrested and face death... I have officers ready to carry out the duty."

They all nodded.

"What about the changing a human into a vampire rule?" Legend questioned.

"That remains the same. If a human is transformed, she or he is to become the mate of that vampire. We still have to be responsible. New vampires are too uncontrollable... Grandfather, I have a question to ask."

"Sure," he replied.

"Am I arranged to marry anyone?"

"No. You are free to marry freely. Are you ready to be married?"

"I'm smitten, but it's not a big deal yet. As everyone in this room knows, I have a colossal appetite for women and I plan on entertaining a lot of them."

Laughter filled the room. I laughed with them.

"You're an available King. You can do whatever you want to. It doesn't matter what any of us say. We can't judge. If you wish to have a hundred women at one time, then that's your business. You are no longer a child," Allemand replied.

"Thank you, Grandfather. Those are the main things I definitely wanted to add. As time goes on, I'll be tweaking things. You all ready to open the club tonight?"

Everyone was on board to make the Grand Opening of Club Azura phenomenal. The meeting was adjourned and everyone went about his or her own business. I took my cell phone and called Nicole. I was able to take a flyer by her house earlier, but she wasn't home, so I left it on the door.

She answered, "Hey you."

"Hey, Nicole. Did you get the flyer?"

"Yes, I did. That was from you?"

"Yeah, it's my family's club. We're opening tonight and I really want to see you there. Come have a drink with me." I smiled into the phone.

"I'll see you there."

"Is it all right if I pick you up?"

"Sure. Can I bring my friends?"

"Of course. Will they behave?"

"Yeah, they will," she said. "I told them all about you. They're intrigued, of course. I made them promise not to tell anyone."

"It's okay if they know. Have you made necklaces for them, too?"

"They made their own... They practice too."

I replied, "No shit. So, I'm going to have a room full of witches?"

She laughed. "No...silly. We aren't witches. We are Enchantresses."

"Got you. I can't wait to see you."

"Same here. I've been thinking about you nonstop."

I felt my dick get hard. "Oh yeah? What you been thinking?"

"I'd rather show you than tell you," she replied. "I'll see you in a few hours."

"All right. I'll see you around ten."

"Okay. I'll be ready," she said.

"Later," I replied.

"Bye."

I ended the call. I left out of the room and walked down the hall. I was going to have to go shopping for something to wear to the Grand Opening, so I had the driver take me.

Flashing spotlights, a brand-new sign highlighted in blue lights, and the line was wrapped around the block. Club Azura was ready for action and the Grand Opening looked like a Hollywood red carpet event. My dad was working the front door and he was wearing his stern face to keep the line from getting too rowdy. I stepped out of the limo with Nicole on my right arm and her three homegirls behind us. She looked so good in that red dress and fishnet stockings.

We stepped into the club and it looked fabulous. I had it decorated with black leather bar stools, couches, and lounge chairs. The blue lighting made it classy, yet gave it a modern feel. It was definitely the place to be that night. I couldn't wait to have stripper nights as soon as the poles would be installed. This place was going to be the "IT" spot for any and everybody.

My mother was at the front door, making sure everyone got stamps on their hands for admittance.

"Hey, son," she said.

"Hey, Mama. This Nicole and her friends, Sasha, Tyra, and Kimora."

"Hello, ladies. Enjoy your night."

"Thank you," they said in unison.

It would've been nice to have all of them at one time, making them all scream out my name with pleasure, but I wasn't worried about having her friends. I only had my eyes on Nicole. Her ass was shaking underneath that dress—it had me staring every time she moved.

We walked to the bar. Legend was working the bar and I was surprised to see Rain on the other side. It was good to see the family doing the things they used to do. I had moved the VIP area upstairs, and got rid of a few of the rooms. We headed up that way and the ladies had a seat on the couch.

I hired a few female vampires to serve drinks in skimpy little outfits and it looked as if everything was all running smoothly. I ordered a few bottles of champagne for my guests. As I looked down at the dance floor, I understood why Azura loved running the club so much. I smiled at her memory. She would've liked to see us like this, working together. I didn't know what the old days were like, but she would've been impressed.

The music was blaring, the beat pounding as bodies grinded on one another. The different hues of blue flashed over the dance floor. I nodded my head to the beat.

A pair of hands wrapped around me. I turned to see Nicole smiling. "This place is fabulous, U."

I liked the way her nickname sounded. It was better that she was the first one to give me a nickname.

"Thank you, baby."

She smiled at me calling her "baby." I licked my lips and sucked on my bottom lip as I peered at her. I was trying to be on my best behavior, but by the heat was coming from her body. We were going to end up fucking before the night was over.

She motioned for me to bend down to her lips. I did what she said and she kissed me. Her friends' eyes were wide with curiosity. Nicole kissed a vampire right in front of them. She wanted to show them that I was harmless. They seemed to be comfortable with being in a place full of vampires. It was made clear that no one would hurt anyone. We were all going to have a good time.

"I want you right now and I don't want to wait," she said. "Is there somewhere we can go?"

I kept the rooms around in case people couldn't wait to get home. I took her hand in mine and led her down the hall to one of the rooms. I had completely redesigned each one. The one I led her to looked like a penthouse suite. I had looked at plenty of magazines to know exactly how I wanted it. It definitely had the feel of luxury. I had cream-colored carpet with a huge black rug in the center of the room. The walls were covered with beautiful canvas paintings of scenery. A plush white loveseat and couch went perfectly with the room. I had intercoms put into each room so we could call down for service if needed. It was a hell of an upgrade.

"This is so nice," she said with a broad grin as she tossed her golden clutch on the coffee table.

"Thank you. I liked to think my aunt is smiling down at all the work I put into this place. I think she would've liked it."

"I'm sure she's smiling down at you right now, feeling so proud."

She licked her lips in anticipation as I invaded her personal space. My hands immediately started traveling all over her body, seeking out every imperfection, every dip, and every curve. My eyes went from her eyes to her lips, from her lips to her breasts, and then from her breasts to her hips. I spun her around to look at her round ass. I palmed it.

She went to the top button of my jeans, jerked it open, revealing the top of my boxers. A moan of pleasure escaped my lips as her hands found their way to my dick. I kissed her hard, my tongue demanded entry into her mouth and she let me in. I moved my hand to the side of her face and traveled down her neck to her shoulders. Her hands never once left the inside of my pants as she stroked me.

I placed my hand on her dress and ripped her fishnet stockings in the center. She looked shocked that I was so rough, but I could tell she liked it. She didn't need to worry about those stockings for the rest of the night. She wasn't going to put them back on cause I was about to tear them apart. She didn't have any panties on so my hand met her wetness. She moaned as my hand went further.

"Nicole," I uttered.

"Yes?"

"I like saying your name."

"I love the way you say my name. I love your voice, period... Your fragrance... Your body..." Her hands went under my shirt and rubbed my muscles. Her hands felt too good.

"What else you love?"

"I love how you exude your power. Your strength and, above all, your desire for me... Your body is so muscular in all the right places. Your height. You don't strike me as egotistical or big-headed, but as the type of man that knows the effect that you have on women."

"Sounds like you love everything about me."

"I do. I also love the effect that I have on you. I do something to you that you've never experienced before. I stir up emotions and feelings that you can't ignore. You're trying to hide it from me."

Nicole was so cute with her pouty lips. I couldn't help but chuckle. I liked how she was telling me how she thought I was feeling. I stared into her eyes and they were like two tiny pools of ecstasy. I could see the depths of them. Her hair hung loose around her face framing it to make her face look softer. I ran my fingers through it to marvel at the texture. Electricity sizzled and sparked between us by the second. I wasn't going to ignore it. Nicole wanted me to solidify exactly what we were doing. Hell, I wanted to know what we were doing.

"You want to date me or something?" I asked.

She placed my hand back between her legs to feel her. "I want you to fuck me right now. We'll talk about dating later."

"Well damn..."

Walking over to the bed, she removed her clothes. She sprawled out on the bed and stretched out. I immediately positioned myself between her legs to taste her.

"You're so fuckin' sexy," she said as she palmed the back of my head.

I licked and sucked her until she could no longer take it.

"Now, you lie down on the bed," she ordered.

I obeyed her. I was her love slave for the night. She wanted to command me as if she were my Queen. She rode me so right that my toes were curling. I had never been fucked that way. I was losing it every time she glided down on me. I was about to cum and I did. I let go into her hot wet center. Her sweaty body collapsed against mine as she had her own orgasm.

We were breathing heavily, staring at one another.

"You're unbelievable, you know that?" I uttered, out of breath.

Nicole wrapped her arms around me as she cuddled up against me. Her warmth and love absorbed me and it made me feel whole. Her warmth was something I could get used to.

After having countless women, I finally felt like I found the perfect woman, my match. She was the only one. The only problem was that she wasn't a vampire. She was so sweet, loving, and sexy, but she was a human. She would grow old and die without me.

As she looked up at me again, her eyes glittered with love. "What are you thinking?" she asked.

"When I met you, I was so confused about the role I was supposed to play. I felt like a lost Prince in a world of nothing but darkness. Nothing really mattered to me much except for having sex with anybody I wanted. I'm the King of Pigalle Palace, a vampire Kingdom, and with you, none of that matters. Being a vampire doesn't even matter to you, does it? Am I a blood-sucking monster?"

"Not at all. You're not a blood-sucking monster to me."

"I think I'm falling in love with you."

Our lips met and passion burned inside of me.

"I feel the same way about you and yes, I would love to date you."

"Even though I'm a vampire?"

"That's what I love most about you." As she said those words, her face had gone from lusty and sinful to beautiful and loving.

She now had the softest part of me.

"One day, you'll grow older than me. I'll always stay the same age forever. What do you think about that?"

"I think that you should make me into a vampire too."

"A lot changes when you become what I am."

"I know that."

"I'm sure you wouldn't want to give up your Enchantress practices..."

"Giving that up wouldn't be an issue for me. I want to learn all there is to know about you and your family. I don't want to date you and fall in love while growing older. I don't want to die without you. That would be torture."

"Let me ask you this," I said as I played with her hair. "What about your family? They won't be able to see you ever again once you change."

"I'm the younger of two siblings. They are nearly twenty years older than I am. My parents had me late in life. Our parents died from old age when I was nineteen. I'm twenty-five now... I've been alone all this time. Family would never be an issue for me."

I studied her eyes and she was serious. She only wanted to become a vampire because of me.

"Let's date for a while. You'll come and hang out at the Château. You'll know all there is to know about being a vampire. Then, if you still want to become one, I'll do it. Once you become one, you'll be my Queen."

"I will be Queen?" she asked with a look as if she hadn't thought about that.

"Yes. How does that make you feel?"

"I'm not sure. I don't mind going from dating to being your girl-friend to being your fiancée and then being your wife. I mean, that's what normal people do."

I smiled at her. I liked the sound of that. I liked how I felt when I was around her. Nicole was definitely someone special from the moment I laid eyes on her.

"We shall do whatever makes us happy."

"What if...what if I said that I was ready to be your Queen right now?"

I studied her. "Only if you mean it."

She took a deep breath. "I mean it. I'm ready. I want to be yours forever."

Those words were the sexiest words I had ever heard. I couldn't imagine having anyone else as my Queen. I embraced her for a few moments before I kissed her neck gently. I read her mind and her thoughts. She was looking forward to being by my side for eternity.

"Do it, U," she demanded.

I opened my mouth wide and I bit down on her neck. I released my venom before sucking her dry. Nicole's transformation began.

ABOUT THE AUTHOR

Niyah Moore is an award-winning author with more than twenty published works to her credit. A Sacramento, California native, Niyah's love affair with the written word began early. By the age of nine, she was fully immersed in the possibilities of prose. Under the subtle urging and guidance of her literary mentors, Niyah embarked on a professional writing career.

A true contemporary artist, Niyah's foray into the literary world began in 2007 with the social media platform Myspace, where she submitted her writing to be included in select anthologies. Niyah has since secured multiple independent publishing deals, as well as having been included in several anthologies such as: Zane's *Busy Bodies: Chocolate Flava 4*, Anna J's *Lies Told in the Bedroom, Heat of the Night*, and *Mocha Chocolate: Taste a Piece of Ecstasy*.

Niyah has a special way with words, which keeps her romance readers, as well as her contemporary fiction fans, anticipating new arrivals. Her noteworthy novels include: *Major Jazz, Guilty Pleasures, Bittersweet Exes, Tell Yo Bitch* series, *Suckcess* series, *Nobody's Side Piece* series, and *Beneath the Bayou*. Niyah was an honoree for the 2013 Exceptional Women of Color Award of Northern California. She is a two-time recipient of the African American Literary Award for Best Anthology, in addition to having won Best Script at the Lenaea Festival.

In 2014, Niyah signed her first major two-book publishing deal with Simon & Schuster, under *New York Times* Bestselling Author Zane's imprint, Strebor Books. Niyah's first release under Strebor Books was *Pigalle Palace*, which was featured by Ebony.com.

After seven years of self-publishing and honing her craft, Niyah stepped into the role of CEO and Publisher launching Ambiance Books in February 2015. Ambiance Books has signed eleven authors to date. Niyah's journey has been paved with determination and drive. She earned a Mass Media Communications degree as well as an Advanced Theater Arts degree from California State University, Sacramento. Niyah's mantra is: *The biggest adventure you can take is to live the life of your dreams.*

This busy businesswoman can be found spending quality time with her husband and children when she is not indulging in a little reality television drama, for inspiration purposes, of course.

IF YOU MISSED HOW IT ALL GOT STARTED,
BE SURE TO PICK UP

PIGALLE PALACE

BY NIYAH MOORE
AVAILABLE FROM STREBOR BOOKS

CHAPTER 1

LEGEND

S he clutched my back, digging her nails into me every time I thrust into her. I loved giving every woman I chose the ultimate pleasure and I couldn't stop from thinking about how good she felt as her sticky walls hugged me. Sinking my teeth into her skin was the other thing that came to my mind, but I didn't want to suck her blood…not yet anyway. I actually hadn't made up my mind if I wanted to feed off her. Her sex seemed satisfying enough not to, and my vampire instincts weren't pulling me in that direction.

After a few more deep long pumps from me, she drew in deep shallow breaths, let go of the death grip she had on my back, and thanked God aloud for one hell of an orgasm.

"Are you okay?" I asked her after I watched her mild trembles subside.

"I'm fine," she exasperated with her eyes wide in amazement.

"Would you like anything else tonight?"

She played in my dreads as she admired my body with her free hand. "Can you make me another Lemon Drop?"

At the bar, earlier that evening, she and her best friend had indulged in the drinks I served them. As a bartender, I met beautiful women by the dozens every night. Most of the faces were familiar, and on occasion, tourists showed up.

"Your Lemon Drop is coming right up." I eased off her.

When she smiled at me, I thought she was stunning, too cute for words. I thought that about her all night long. Before I brought her home from Club Vaisseau, I admired her honey-colored skin, medium-brown, doe-like eyes, and long dark hair from the other side of the bar.

I recognized any type of freak, regardless of what type of clothing she wore. This one was so freaky that she allowed me to sex her before even knowing her name. Typical for me, though. One-night stands weren't a rare event on my calendar. I needed many women to quench my desire for sex the way quarts of blood satisfied my hunger.

I draped my bare body in a bathrobe. "Mademoiselle, pardon me, but what's your name?"

She giggled sexily, yet I could tell that she, too, felt embarrassed about not exchanging that information earlier. "Chantal."

"You're really beautiful, Chantal. It's been a pleasure having your company tonight."

She blushed and stammered, "T-t-t-hanks."

"Don't move, and um, keep those clothes off." Holding up my index finger, I signaled for her to wait while I went downstairs to make her another Lemon Drop.

Chantal giggled again, the way a schoolchild did when told a dirty joke. She didn't have to play the shy role anymore. I had already gotten what I needed from her, but my mere presence had her still feeling shy. Hell, it made all women act that way whenever they were around me. That was my gift and my curse—to capture a woman effortlessly.

I swiftly made her sweet lemon concoction, and was back upstairs in a flash.

"You move fast," she said with a bright smile.

All vampires moved fast. However, she hadn't noticed my fangs because I hid them well around humans. I only revealed them when I was ready to drink. By then, the hypnotic state masked my intentions.

I handed her the Lemon Drop while my eyes peered down at her curvy body.

"Thank you, Mr. ...?"

I hadn't told her my name, either.

"Please, call me Legend."

"Legend? Is that your real name?"

"It's the only name I know."

She stared at me oddly, as she took a few sips from the glass. "I have to pee." As she got up from the bed, her thick hips grazed against me.

I grunted lowly, while falling back on the bed, feeling happy with having her over for the night.

When she finished relieving her bladder, she asked, "Legend?"

"What's up, Chantal?"

"How come your skin is so cold?" She stood in front of the bed with a look of bewilderment.

"My skin is cold?" I repeated as if I didn't know that I wasn't warm-blooded.

Warm blood hadn't run through me for over a century.

She hesitated as her eyes glanced over me nervously. I could tell her mind was trying to put the pieces together and recollect if she'd noticed any other strange things throughout the evening.

Chantal had come to the bar with her friend, and whether or not they were aware, it was no accident how they'd ended up in Pigalle Palace or even in the Red Light District, for that matter. The Red Light District was devoted to prostitution and other illegal, immoral behavior. The Red Light District was heavy in sexual acts.

Therefore, our meeting was no accident.

Whether pussy was bought, sold, or given freely, it was our haven nonetheless.

Our popular thriving nightclub, Vaisseau, was one of the many notorious hotspots. Pigalle Palace was an epicenter of sizzling sex shops, erotic peep shows, and dazzling strip clubs. It was an adults-only, X-rated pleasurable adventure for the more risqué crowd and home to one of Paris' most famous cabarets, the Moulin Rouge.

This was our playground and Chantal was having a ball. In the back of her mind, she had already known what I was and that excited her.

Speechless for a second, she finally replied, "Now that I'm thinking about it, from the moment your lips touched mine at the club, I noticed. I noticed something different about you all night. I've heard many things about Pigalle Palace. Let me say that you were the one that catapulted my curiosity further. I finally got to touch *one* up close and very personal."

"One of what?"

A quick frown appeared on her face, yet she continued, "Are you going to bite me now?"

What had me confused was that she looked as if she were disap-pointed that I hadn't taken a bite out of her yet. "You want me to bite you?"

Chantal straddled me and ran her feather-feeling hands across my chest. "Am I not worthy enough?"

"Are you not worthy enough to be killed?"

Her eyes widened with fear. "Oh no, no, no. I don't want you to kill me. Are you going to kill me? I hope you don't kill me…"

"What do you want from me, Chantal?"

"I want you to turn me into what it is that you are."

The way her eyes sparkled when she suggested such a ridiculous thing made me stare deeply into her eyes. I wasn't going to hypnotize or compel her. I simply didn't know many humans that wanted to become what we were. Hell, we didn't want to either, but we had no other choice.

"I'm very careful and *we* don't change anyone unless it's discussed amongst the family first."

"Have you ever changed anyone behind their backs?"

I got very serious on her. "Legend follows all rules."

"Is that the only reason why you haven't taken my blood, Legend?"

Instantly, I wanted to kill her. When she mentioned blood, it triggered my hunter instincts, and I wanted to suck her until she became lifeless.

I dismissed the urge. "You don't want me to answer that."

She gasped with fascination. "Can I see your fangs?"

I tilted my head back a bit so she could see what she was begging for.

"Wow. Legend, you are truly a vampire. My assumption was correct all along."

"And now that you've proven your theory to be correct, what do you want to do?"

I could feel the heat pulsating from her moist center that greeted me so pleasantly. She was excited by her discovery and was ready to open up her body for me again. To be honest, I was turned on as well, but I had to see where she wanted to go with this.

"I want you to have me."

"I've already had you, Chantal."

"Drink from me." She put her wrist up to my nose.

Though she smelled so delicious, I gently lowered her arm and explained, "I've been a vampire for a very long time. This is my destiny, not yours. You should enjoy the fact that you're still alive."

She swallowed hard and thought about that for a moment, but then she was right back to trying to pressure me. "You sure you don't want to bite me?" She tossed her hair over her shoulder to reveal her neck. I spotted a luscious thick vein that I could have devoured if I'd truly wanted to.

"I'm sure."

The urge to bite her surged through me the same way my adrenaline had my blood rushing, but I had self-control.

"Why not?" She began plastering kisses on the side of my face.

"Stop it," I said in a demanding tone.

She backed away with a look of confusion, pushing her hair out of her face with one hand.

My family didn't have a choice. We were born with this curse.

My right eye pulsated as it fluttered. A painful migraine formed. Out of the corner of my eye, I could see Chantal staring at me before sauntering over to the window to look down at the city of Montmartre.

"Oh my... This is a sight to see. I've never seen this side of Paris before..."

I had an excellent panoramic view of the city and it was breathtaking.

"We're on a hill, north of Paris, one hundred thirty metres high."

"The city is so beautiful, Legend."

I got up from the bed and wrapped my arms around her waist. The thought of slipping back inside of her came to mind. Without any distractions, I would be able to enjoy her for a little while longer before the sun would come up. She would then go on her merry little way and her fantasy of spending a complete night with a vampire would be fulfilled.

She twirled around to face me. Her eyes shifted down while sadness seemed to consume her. She was curious about becoming something she didn't understand. Our world was dark and confusing to most, yet she was so ready.

"I've read plenty of vampires' tales and stories."

"That's fiction. I'm real and trust me when I say that you're better off."

"Maybe I should leave."

I stopped her with my voice—smooth, gentle, and reassuring. "Chantal, I'm not done with you, yet. Unless, you're afraid of me now."

"I'm not afraid... Do you always have your way?"

"Always," I stated into the thickened air.

"You sure you don't want to sink your teeth into me? I think I might taste very good."

Her hands moved over my muscles as if she were trying to memorize everything about me.

My hands then moved to her lower back. She closed her eyes as her breathing became heavier. I listened intently, pulling her back to rest up against me while my hands felt around her firm ass. Her breathing grew even heavier with a hint of arousal as my fingertips traveled between her legs to rub her clit. I turned her around, face to face, to inhale her sweet-smelling breath as I inched toward her. I grabbed her firmly, pulled her up against me, and kissed her.

I sucked her neck and then her collarbone, making a suction trail as I led her back to the bed. I pushed her onto her back. She didn't object as I went down to please her. My lips met her warm wetness. She moaned as I sucked her hungrily.

Her low moan began to rise each time I licked her juicy clit. I picked up my slow pace to a moderate rate, feeling her juices squirt and then ooze down between her thighs. I lapped every drop because she tasted that good. By then, she had both fists full of my dreads.

I palmed her ass and squeezed her while her eyes closed tightly. Suddenly her moans stopped and she said, "Ahhhh… Ouch."

As I tasted her blood, I realized I had pierced her inner lips.

"Shit." I tried to get up, but she palmed the back of my head with both of her hands.

"Don't stop… Keep going… Do it."

Without thinking about anything else, I returned my face between her thighs and sucked her blood. Biting her wasn't my intention, but she had aroused me in a way that had me feeling as if I had no control over myself.

Transforming her was something she wanted anyway, so I released my venom and wiped my bloody mouth.

As she had another orgasm, the transformation began. Once her body was done with twisting and writhing in a frantic manner, her sweaty body slid away from me. She didn't cuddle next to me or whisper sweet things as if she loved me for what she'd asked of me all along. Instead, she turned away from me.

I watched her back rise and fall gently as she breathed acutely. I ran my fingers over my dreads as regret washed over me. *What had I done?*

Chantal asked, "How come you couldn't just bite my neck the way I've seen in movies?"

"I wasn't trying to bite you."

"What happens now?"

"The sun will rise. If you decide to walk outside, the sun will touch your skin and you will burn."

She glimpsed over at the window and panicked. "Are you going to close the curtains? I don't want to burn."

"My windows are actually UV protected. You are safe in my home."

A series of electrifying chills shot straight up my spine, creating goose bumps all over my body. I shook the snake-like feeling, heaved a heavy sigh, and closed myself in the bathroom.

My family didn't care about how many women I let into my bed, but the rules were made out to be simple: one was that I could only change one and one only. That one would be my wife for eternity. Those were actually the rules of the covenant. My parents didn't make up those rules. The covenant was made up of laws set by the Préfet—the vampire government of Pigalle Palace.

Before I could gather my thoughts, my phone rang from the countertop of the bathroom. I forgot that I had left it there when I showered. It was my sister, Azura, calling.

My whole family had the gift of premonition. Azura's was the strongest. I knew why she was calling.

"Hello," I answered.

"What are you up to?" Azura asked.

"Nothing much," I tried to elude her.

"Are you planning on leaving home anytime soon?"

"No. The sun will be coming up in a few hours, so I'm in for the night."

"Mother and Father want to see you."

I closed my eyes as I knew exactly why they wanted to see me. "When?"

"Right now."

"Right now?"

"Yes, Legend, right now! Onyx and Rain are already here."

My brothers were already there, so they were aware of what I had done. I was going to have to face them, but I didn't think it would be this soon.

"I'll be there in a moment."

"Hurry," she answered quickly. "Oh, and bring *her* with you."